Janan Jubedottir

by
Ben Houser

PUBLISH AMERICA

PublishAmerica
Baltimore

First printing

ISBN: 1-4137-5735-9
PUBLISHED BY PUBLISHAMERICA, LLLP
www.publishamerica.com
Baltimore

Printed in the United States of America

For Jen and Rob

Foreword

"It was just after the latest battle for the Gempore Plain, and the war leader, Antore, had some minor but irritating wounds. To salve his irritation he brutalized Janan, his favorite captive camp follower; one of her rivals had whispered in his ear of Janan's pregnancy. When she could no longer even crawl, he threw her out of the tent and ordered the camp struck. He would move north to solidify his gains and plan the next attack."

An old, old man sat on a stool by the flame. Those seated around the fire pit in the village plaza gave the old teller of tales their full attention. "This be the start of the tale I tell, of Janan Jubedottir."

One

A hot sun was bearing down when she woke, and she hurt all over. Squinting through her one usable eye, Janan rolled her head slowly from side to side and looked at her only company, buzzards eyeing her from a dead tree. Finally she rolled on her side, then, groaning, she pushed her way to her knees.

Nothing is more desolate than a hurriedly deserted campsite. All there was to see were smoking fire pits, trash and a few castoffs. Janan almost gave up, but before she had been dragged from her home and given to the war leader, Antore, she was daughter to a strong man. A hunter, Jube had taught his daughter much of weapons and the wildwood before the war rolled over their small community.

Slowly coming to her feet, she talked encouragement to herself. "No, you don't, girl. Jube's girl doesn't quit. First you had better visit that bathing pool below the falls." At the sound of her raspy voice, the vultures took flight.

After the battered girl had soaked in the sun-warmed pool, she washed herself and her clothing as best she could. Wringing out her gown, she put it on and limped back to the campsite. While the gown dried on her back, she scavenged for food. Using the long stick she had found in the wood by the pool, she beat off other scavengers and was surprised at the amount of food scattered around.

While looking for food, Janan found a large bent and battered pot to carry it in. A smaller pot had a hole in it, but it sufficed to carry coals from one of the fire pits. Carrying the food and a few torn and dirty articles of clothing, she searched for and found a small shallow cave near the falls. After building a good fire in the entrance, she threw fire into the cave until sure it held no surprises. The larger pot she settled in the sand of the cave's floor and covered the pot's opening with a big, flat rock. After rebuilding the fire, she headed back to the campsite.

On her return from scavenging, she cooked and ate a meal, then worked on her weapon. Janan knew the fire was a beacon to bring trouble, but it would keep away all animals except for the two-legged kind. For that animal she used the belt knife to make a shaft for the spearhead she had found. It was a rough life on the frontier, but the weapon instruction she had received from her father just might keep her alive.

The next morning she was almost too stiff and sore to climb from her nest of evergreen boughs and long grasses, but hunger forced her to make the effort. The food stuffs were getting old, but a stew, cooked long enough, would not make her sick. When she found a place to settle she could rig snares and dead-falls for meat. Wild fruit, roots and greens were plentiful.

"Well, girl," Janan mumbled over her stew, "you are in trouble. You can make it on your own, but later you will need some help. I don't think you lost Antore's whelp to the beating he gave you. For now I guess you better make one more sweep of the campsite, take the best and cache the rest, then get out of here."

She was still a bit wide-eyed—at least in one eye, the other was still swollen shut—at all she had found. The knife was the greatest find. It had fallen from a pair of dirty and ragged trousers she had almost not picked up. When she pulled it from the sheath the blade was bright, sharp and hardly worn. If alive, some warrior was going to be very unhappy with his loss. The spear point she had found half-buried near one of the fire pits. The greatest treasures, though, belonged to her. Always she carried flints and a packet of metal needles in the hidden pocket sewn inside her gown.

Coming back from washing out her battered pot, Janan was reiterating the orders she had given herself. "Check the camp again, then get out of here. This place is too close to the trace, and too close to water. Move, girl, before someone finds you. Time to head for the wood."

Walking slowly and resting often, Janan was two days into her very slow trek through the woods when she made camp in the edge of the Desolation. The bail of the battered pot was trying to pull her arm loose from her shoulder, and her flimsy camp sandals were falling off her feet. "Damn all warriors," she grumbled quietly. Then she said, "This will have to be far enough, for now."

Back at the narrow entrance of the tiny blind canyon, she put together a man-sized dead-fall that would also loose a good-sized rock fall. Satisfied with her defenses, she went back to check the pool of water. The small stream that fed the pool came out of a hole in the rock. Where it left the pool, the water disappeared down another crack in the rock.

Plugging the hole in the smaller pot with a peg, she used it to fill the larger pot. While the water heated, she located some soap root at the verge of the pool. There was a patch of lavender growing far back in the canyon. Janan nodded and said, "Good enough. Not soap, but close enough for a good cleanup. Me first, then the pickings from the campsite."

Early the third morning of her stay in the canyon she heard her man trap let go. Armed with spear and belt knife, she moved carefully toward the narrow entrance, taking advantage of all possible cover. From behind a large rock she studied the fallen trap and the area around it; nothing was moving. Slowing her approach even more, she moved like a shadow from cover to cover, ending up at a place she could look down on the trap. Then she relaxed; half a deer rack was showing from under the debris.

It was a chance she took, but Janan put up a smoker made of evergreen branches. It was a chance, but it would be very unwise of anyone to follow the smokey trail; the man trap had been rebuilt. As she worked at smoking the meat and brain-tanning the deer hide, she kept the spear at her side.

After she had been in her small canyon for a full moon, Janan was ready to move on. She had two eyes working again, though the one was still tender and probably colored. The snug trousers she wore had been cut down from someone's castoffs, and were mostly patches, as was her sleeveless shirt. Little was left of the scavenged clothing, just various-sized rags, but she had useful clothing now. Her gown, cleaned and dried, was rolled in those rags and stowed in the large pot. The pot rested in the reed-woven basket that was attached to the pack frame she had made. The reeds had also provided a sun hat and thick soles for the sandals she wore. The sandal straps had come from the flimsy, ruined camp sandals. Shoulder straps and pads for the pack were made of braided trouser material. She grinned at her own puffed-up pride in herself; she was doing all right.

Being very careful, Janan did not push her pace even though she knew her destination. Taking time for the tanning of hides and the making of a water skin, she added to her survival needs. By the time she had been discarded the battle had moved quite far to the south. Now that the battle had moved back north, she felt safe in returning to the village she had called home all her life.

Keeping to the edge of the Desolation, she moved slowly south. With her water skin always full, she knew she could fade into the Desolation and be safe; this was her country. The demarcation was surprisingly abrupt. The edge of the Desolation was almost solid rock. The woodland spread shade where the rock gave way to soil. The woodland held food and water, and the Desolation held safety…of a sort.

The Desolation was dry country. High and sheer and broken hills, heat, sand and rock…and all knew that was all it held. Her father was the exception. He had more than once searched for, and found, children lost in that wilderness of heat and boulders. He was a hunter and could track even in that trackless waste; once he had found something he confided only to his daughter.

Roots, fruit and greens were plentiful, as was small game. Janan now wore soft boots of tanned hare hides that kept her rough sandals from scouring her feet and ankles. Deer were plentiful, so her pack now held smoked meat and the tanned and rolled hides. She too was tanned, by sun and wind, and her strength had grown by lengths and bounds. She was once more Janan Jubedottir.

Three moons after she had been thrown out of Antore's tent, Janan spotted the landmark she was looking for. Filling the water skin, she moved into the Desolation. Her memory did not fail her. The huge boulder overlooking the small village was right on the southern boundary of the Desolation, where her memory told her it would be, but the village was not.

Her bleak glance took in the scene below the overlook. The black patches, marking where huts had once stood, were fading. Tall weeds grew among stones that had been walls. As she lay on the hard rock, her face was almost as stony as the boulder. Then she lowered her face to her forearm and let the tears come; her home was gone. Where was her father? Where were all the villagers? Were they all dead?

She lay still for a long time, an uncaring time that went on and on, then there were sounds in the woods to the east. When she raised her head she saw what could only be a group of army scouts riding from the trees. Still flat on her stomach, she moved back a little and watched the horsemen come into the clearing below, then a company of foot soldiers moved out of the trees. The foot were soon at work setting up a camp. When Janan saw a familiar tent being raised she realized it was time to go. If Antore found her…

Slipping off the overlook, she put on the pack and looped the strap of the water skin over her head to rest the bag on the hip opposite the shoulder it hung from. Grabbing her spear, she moved out at a ground-covering, silent lope, heading north into the Desolation. She might need help, but there was no help in that tent. Then again, women had birthed alone before this.

Two

Other than stopping to find high vantage points to check her backtrack, she moved at a ground-covering run. Walking to rest from her running, she would then go back to the easy lope she had learned as a girl.

When the sun was on the horizon, Janan slowed her pace. "Jube said it would be five leagues north and a little west." She was grumbling under her breath. "He didn't say how far west or how many days, though."

The Desolation was supposed to be without dangerous wildlife, but she was taking no chances. As she built a rock wall to enclose the small overhung niche in a bluff, she mumbled, "No fire tonight, girl. No wood, anyway. I should have gathered sticks as I went." She knew the small dry country bush, known as oil-wood, burned hot and nearly smoke-free, but the bushes were few and far between. Not much grew in the Desolation.

She had been keeping watch and had been moving as quietly as she could; Jube had told her of the small desert deer that was the only animal found here. Not only had she not seen such an animal, she had not found even a track of one.

"Huh, don't need a fire; nothing to cook, and I am not wasting water to make a stew of my dried stuff." Janan was grumbling so she could hear something besides the wind as she dug into her store of deer jerky.

The third day she gave in to her longing for something more than dried meat. Putting the pot on a small, hot fire, she added a double handful of various dried roots and leaves, then a small handful of dried fruit. After cutting the dried meat into small pieces as she held it over the pot, she added just enough water to make a thick stew. The wood spoon she had carved while in her first campsite was fine for stirring, but was a poor eating tool.

After emptying the pot, Janan scrubbed it with dry sand until it seemed reasonably clean. Repacking everything, she leaned against the pack and gave a satisfied belch. "Needed something besides jerky, else I might come down with a flux." She belched again and chuckled. "Makes a good excuse for wasting water." *Wonder if talking just to hear a voice means I have been alone too long.* Her low, warm chuckle came again.

The following days were long and, as before, she seemed to be backtracking as much as she was moving forward. She held her pace to a walk, and stayed in the shade of hills and bluffs when she could. The sun and hot, dry wind made her thirsty, and her water supply was limited.

"Just as well head east and replenish my food and water," Janan grumbled aloud while taking a break. She also wondered if she had somehow missed the place her father had told her of. Her seven days in the Desolation had almost emptied her water skin, and the nearest water was to the east at least three leagues. Maybe more. The peaks to the east were a barrier now, sheer and unbroken.

"It might get some thirsty out before I get out of this mess."

As she rested in the shade of a bluff, the faint smell of wood smoke brought her head up and questing into the wind. *Someone else is out here!*

She stood to put on her pack, then headed west only to lose her smokey trail. She turned north until she found it again, then modified her track to the northwest. As she held to all the cover she could find, Janan kept her movements slow and quiet, looking for any trap or lookout guard. The smell was faint, so the fire could be far away.

The wind out of the northwest was light, but steady. The smell was still not strong, but when she topped a low hill she was looking down into a tiny green valley. Quickly moving back the way she had come, Janan got below the crest of the hill and quickly stripped off her pack and water skin. With just her spear and belt knife she belly-walked back to the crest, where she found a good-sized rock to break up her silhouette while she studied the scene below her perch.

The tiny, well-watered valley was divided by a fence of thorns. In the half closest to Janan stood a well-constructed rock hut and well-tended gardens. A good half of the area was planted in maize. Both the maize and the gardens were fed water from a branch that began at the small spring near the hut. The northern half of the valley was pasture and trees. Three dairy animals lay under one tree. Another tree shaded a few goats. Someone was living pretty well. Her pulse jumped—maybe her Da.

There must be some way, some access. Janan was frowning as she studied the lay of the valley. The walls around the valley were sheer except for the occasional cut leading to the valley floor. Each cut ended in a tangle of thorns. *Surely they have a path out of that place!*

As she continued her vigil her hope was dashed when an old man, not her vigorous father, hobbled out of the hut, followed by a ragged old woman. Together they made their way to the garden and picked up some tools. The old man limped to the head of the garden to divert the irrigation flow to another ditch. The old woman filled a basket at a pile of compost.

Probably mixes animal dung with garbage, vegetable tops, weeds, straw, leaves and what-have-you. Water the pile and let it molder for six moons or so, stirring and watering the pile occasionally, then start another pile while she uses the first. In her mind's eye, Janan could see the two piles behind her old home next to the garden there. Watching a few more moments while the woman scattered compost down a row to be planted, she cursed her mind wandering and eased back down the slope of the hill.

First Janan took a good drink of tepid water from the nearly flat water skin, then cached it and the pack in some rocks. Making an unobtrusive four-stone cairn to mark the spot, she checked for landmarks to ease the finding of her treasures, then started around the valley, heading to the north; the possible access she had spotted was on that side of the valley.

Janan was puzzled by the time she reached the cut she was looking for. Already there had been three triggers to ease around, for three rock falls. But the rocks were not set up to fall on whoever triggered the fall; the rocks would have fallen into the valley.

After finding the cut she was looking for, she eased down the small breach in the rock and found a narrow ledge that would bring her within jumping distance of the tree she had spotted from the other end of the valley.

As Janan carefully walked the ledge, she sighed with satisfaction. She could jump to one big limb and grab the smaller limb above it. Then she spotted the tree-mounted trigger. Again she was puzzled. If she was in the tree, the rocks would miss hitting her. A further study showed her something else. If she had moved on down the ledge she would have triggered the rocks down on her head. Devious!

Back on top, Janan carefully removed the rocks that were set to fall, taking the trigger rock last. As she worked, she finally resolved the puzzle. The sound of rocks banging down the walls would echo all around the valley. An intruder alarm! She had been very lucky.

As she ran toward the break in the thorn fence, Janan cursed steadily under her breath. When she landed on the large limb, the trigger sticks had fallen, but no rock followed. When she grabbed the small limb above, rocks on down the way fell with a rumble. And the sound had echoed around the valley. Not that the rocks were really needful, her appearance in the pasture started the bleating of those be-damned goats; that was warning enough.

When Janan slid through the wood bars that comprised the gate to the pasture, she found the other half of the valley deserted. *Damn, the old folk moved faster than I thought they could. Now what?* She could almost feel eyes tracking her as she walked to the open space before the hut. Stopping well out of arrow reach, she put both hands on the spear and leaned on it.

As she waited she pulled the brim of her sun hat low and peered through the afternoon sunlight at the hut. If they had a longbow, they might be able to corner her before she could get out of the valley. *Guess I'll have to talk fast. I need to stay here. I* have *to stay here!*

Finally there was movement in the doorway of the hut. The man limped slowly into the sunlight, longbow and nocked arrow at ready. "Who are you and how did you find this place?"

Janan stared at the face of the man. Her heart swelled to choke off her voice, and tears blurred her vision. She coughed to clear her throat, and blinked to clear her eyes; her voice was raspy. "Who do you know, Jube, that would walk five leagues into the Desolation without knowing there was water to be had?"

The man just stared at her until she said, "Who else, but a Jubedottir?" She swept her hat off. "…You old he-goat!"

"Janan?" Jube squinted his eyes, then exclaimed, "Janan!" Dropping his weapons, he limped toward her. "Janan, is it really you, girl?"

She met him halfway and, dropping her spear, wrapped her arms around him. "Da, Da, oh, Da, I thought you were dead. I thought all were dead." Then she noticed the top of his head just came to the level of her chin. Could she have grown that much in just two years?

She let him go and stepped back, but he held to her hands. Squinting up at her face, he said, "You have grown some, girl."

"Aye, up and around." Janan looked over her father's head to see who spoke, and saw a woman standing just outside the hut, another longbow in her hands. Why had she thought the two of them old? Then she noted the rags the woman wore, and thought of her father's limp.

"Megan, you don't know how glad I am to see you."

She saw the glint of humor in the older woman's eyes. "Aye, and I doubt not that you will be even gladder about four or five moons from now."

Janan grinned at her. "Nearer to four, Meg. At least that is what I make it."

"What be you women yammerin' about?"

"Never mind, Da." She picked up her spear and nodded toward the

16

hut. "I think I would like to get out of this sun, then drink about half my weight of cool water and eat something besides jerky. Then," she said, checking for landmarks and pointing, "get up there. I have some things cached just over that hill."

Three

When she followed Megan into the hut, Janan was impressed. There was a fireplace with irons and a rock chimney. To the left of that, with its own chimney, bulked the round shape of a beehive oven. On the right was a big mattress made of straw-stuffed doe skin, and there were a goodly number of shelves made of rock and woven willow limbs.

Janan had her fill of cool water, but the meal had to be cooked. For that the beehive oven had to be fired up. "Baked or flame-cooked is all we got, girl." Meg was stirring up the fire below the heat chamber of the oven. Janan grinned when she added, "Oh, for just one pot!"

"Well, then, if you will show me a way out of this hole, Da, I will go up and collect my treasures. Every path out of this place seems to be blocked by thorn."

Jube chuckled. "If you were on the hill you pointed to you were right on top of the place you were lookin' for. Come along, girl, and you can get what's hid up there."

Jube led her to a cut that was blocked by a thick growth of wicked spiked thorns. Grinning at her frown, he pulled two long poles out of the matted thorn. One pole had a stub of a limb still attached. With that, he hooked the matted thorns and pulled. When he had pulled the mat aside, a prickly tunnel was revealed.

"When you come back, say 'Jubedottir,' and I'll let you back in."

Careful not to get close to the thorns, she moved through the barrier, then turned to watch the closing of the gateway. When Jube finished pushing, poking and prodding the thorn gate back into position, Janan could not see where gate began and the rest of the thorn ended.

Turning away, she moved on uphill to a place she could spot the marker she had left, but did not go down to retrieve her pack. Instead, Janan kept below the ridge as she moved toward the higher part of the hill and another big, silhouette-destroying rock. From that vantage point she looked back down the way she had first come to the hill. She could see a good way before a bluff blocked her view. Her track was visible for several rods, but Janan noted the wind was already at work; her prints would soon be gone.

When Janan returned, Jube opened the "gate" for her. After passing through the thorn-lined tunnel she watched him stuff the matted thorn back into the passage. When satisfied, he rammed first one pole then the other at a slant through the plug and into the main thorn mat. Grinning, he said, "Ain't nobody comin' through that."

Back in the hut they found Meg shaping ground maize into three good-sized pones of bread. While Meg used her bread paddle to insert the pones into the oven, Janan eased off her pack. Taking four rolls of well-tanned deer hides out of the pack, she threw them to Jube.

"They might be in need of more work, Da, but they should do for the making of some buckskins; both of us could use a new rig-out."

While Jube shook out one of the hides, Janan reached into the pack and came out with the little pot. Megan, who had come up behind the younger woman, took the pot right out of her hands.

"Got a hole in it, Meg, but it might be of some use if we can find a way to patch it."

"Aye, we could make tea in it; beats what we got now. Now we use hot rock to heat the water, a real pain in the neck."

"You have tea!"

"Yep. Jube has worked on this place for years, and we did more after we settled in. He had a lot of stuff here, like tea bush, but nary a pot or pan, and not enough metal to make one."

Jube threw the hide on the bed and took the pot over by the light at the doorway. After a careful examination, he nodded. "Yep, I think I got just the thing for a patch. Heat 'em both up and hammer-weld 'em. What else you got in that pack, girl?"

Janan reached in and brought out the roll of rags. Unrolling the bundle, she shook out the gown. "I think we can cut this down for you, Meg. I don't want it, and you look in need." As the older woman examined the treasure, Janan added, "Look in the left side and see what is in the little pocket I sewed there."

When she had loosed the ties of the little leather packet and unrolled it, Megan stared a long time, touching the dozen or so needles with a fingertip. Carefully she re-rolled the packet and retied the leather ties, then turned to Janan and put her arms around the taller girl. There were tears in her eyes when she looked up.

"Girl, if you only knew…" a tear spilled over, to run down one cheek, "…how much I have wanted a decent gown." She stepped back and gestured at her ragged dress. "Jube made me a needle out of a thorn and burned an eye in it, but it makes for crude sewing, and I have to pull thread from the hem."

"Well," said Janan as she reached to brush the tear from Meg's cheek, "when we cut this gown down to size we will have plenty left over to pull thread from.

"And I have one more thing," Janan said, reaching into the shadows where her pack sat. As she searched for the bale of the larger pot, she continued. "I think my last treasure will be more than welcome."

While Meg was happily making a stew of garden truck and dried meat, Jube and Janan found comfortable seating on the bed. "What took you so long, girl? I thought yer stuff was just over that hill."

"Checked out my backtrack, Da. I have been doing that about three times a day. I came into the Desolation from the south end, from the village, and I have been walking seven days. I thought you said it was just five leagues."

"Eh, eh, eh." Jube squinted his eyes as he chuckled. "It is, girl, it is…if you know the way." Then he sobered. "Had I known we would have needed this place so soon, I would have give you better direction.

Now then, where you been all this time? What happened to you? Our folk headed west and just kept goin', by the sign. We don't know how far they went, or if they even got to where they were headed. I could hardly walk when Old Meg found me, so…"

"Who you calling old, you old goat." Meg grinned from her place by the fire.

Janan smiled at the nonsense, but her expression changed as she began her tale. "I got caught waiting for you, Da, and ran into our hut. Figured I could go out the back way and into the wood. It didn't work, though. There were already warriors in the garden. Before I could even try to hide, two came in the front and dragged me out to the plaza. Figured they would do me right there, but their war chief claimed me and turned me over to this big eunuch he had in his train. That son of a dog put a leash on me and dragged me along behind a wagon that held the warlord's truck. When they made camp and put up Antore's tent, the eunuch took me in and hitched me to the tent pole. After Antore had his supper, and a talk with his lead warriors, he ran everyone out of the tent and raped me. I was always kept by that be-damned eunuch, and when I would not cooperate, Antore just raped me again. When I got my hands on his knife and tried to kill him, he beat me up and raped me again. Finally, the other two women in his train talked to my head. They told me that if I gave him too much trouble he would throw me to his men, so I played along, hoping I could find a way to escape. When he found that I was pregnant, he beat me senseless and left me for dead. I woke in a deserted campsite, and it took me near three moons to get shaped up and back to the village."

Jube's face was expressionless. "I will kill him."

"No, Da, I will kill him. Even if he wins this war of his and makes himself a king, some day I will kill that dog's get."

It was quiet in the stone hut until after Meg had served up the stew in fired clay bowls. Janan broke open her hot pone of bread and put butter on each side. While the butter soaked in, she turned to Jube. "What of you two? How did just the two of you end up here?"

Jube shrugged. "Mathou and me spotted them comin' and was tryin' to get to the village ahead of them when two of their scouts jumped us.

After us put them out of their misery, I had this little leg wound, so I told Mathou to go on ahead and warn our folk. By the time I got there the place was burned to the ground."

Megan's smile was grim. "Back in the Desolation, I had this little, dry cave where I stored some of my herbs. A lot of rumors were floating around about this war, so I had been putting a few extras in the cave. I didn't figure I could run all that fast, and I figured I could hide out there if something went awry. When Mathou came running in, and everyone was loading up and heading west into the wildwood, I grabbed some water skins and food and headed for my cave. I dragged an old rug behind me, so I didn't leave any tracks. When things got quiet I snuck back to that big overlook rock. Way off, I could see some of those warriors coming back—I figured they were sent back to rob the gardens—and there was old Jube sitting in the plaza, trying to fix his leg. Well, I dragged him back to my cave, patched up his leg, then had to get him healed when he caught a fever from where he got stabbed. After things settled down, and Jube got a little stronger, we tried to find our people. We couldn't go far, and from the look of things they just kept going. Anyway, warriors and deserters kept popping back into the village clearing, and we figured we better hop on out of there before we got ourselves caught. Jube told me about this place, and since we had scavenged about all we could from the village, we headed out. We watched for you, Jan, when we made trips to my cave. We finally emptied that cave but never saw hide nor hair of you. We didn't know if you were dead or alive, and we were in no shape to go a-looking."

"So they lose their village and their healer."

"Huh," Meg grunted. "Just as well. Jube needed me worse than they did, and now you need me. What were you planning to do out here by yourself?"

"Drop that whelp, strangle it and get about my business!"

The healing woman gave her a wintry little smile. "Well, now you won't need to do that. I am here to help, and if you don't have the milk, we have those goats."

"What makes you think I want him?"

"Well, for one thing, mine will need some company to grow up with."

22

"Yours?"

"Yep. I wouldn't let Jube in my bed until he said the words. Ever since we have been trying to make a babe. I think we finally made one."

"Wouldn't have been my fault if you didn't, old girl. I were beginnin' to think you didn't have a young'n left in yer hide."

"Huh, you old he-goat. If you got the man left in you, I'll make you two or three."

Janan chuckled at their antics, then said, "I will think about it, but I don't know that I want any of Antore's get."

Jube stood, frowning at his daughter. "Won't be Antore's, will be Jananson."

Four

"So, girl, do you want to throttle them now or later?"

Janan smiled at the older woman, then, dipping her chin, she smiled down on the twins as they worked at getting their first meal.

Glancing back to Megan's smiling face, she gave a tired grin. "'Taint a whelp, Meg; they be Janandottir. I think we better keep them, but…" she frowned down at the small heads, "…they have no hair."

"That would not be unusual, girl, but they do have hair. It is there, but the hair is so fine and lacking in color you can hardly see it. Just may be a pair of white heads."

Coming through the doorway, Jube heard Meg's speculation. "Na, na, old girl." He stared at the twins. "Yaller, like Jan's grandma, maybe. Are you gals all done making babies?"

"Aye, old goat." Megan handed him a bound cloth that had been anointed with an aromatic herbal. "And here is the package for the altar. Make your prayer for two young ladies."

***

Megan sat under the sun shade that roofed the area before the third hut, where she could listen for Minna's call. Min was near her time.

The cool of the morning was set aside for weapons training, the

24

afternoon for chores and schooling. Janan insisted that the twins learn their letters and numbers. Megan's boy joined them in all the schooling.

Under the tutelage of Jube, the fourteen-year-old twins were working with spears. "Na, na, na, ladies, remember the shaft, remember the shaft! If you depend on the point only you lose half the power of yer weapon. Here, Deeta, give me yer spear and stand back and watch. Now, Leeta, come at me."

When Leeta charged her grandfather with her headless spear, Jube met her weapon with his, deflected the point to pass over his head, then swatted her behind with the butt of his spear.

"Now then, Lee, if that had been for real, I'd have thumped you alongside yer hard head, or broke an arm, maybe a leg, or maybe used it to crush yer windpipe." He turned to a dummy and demonstrated.

"Now you can rest a while. Work with yer longbows while yer old grandpa sets a spell."

Janan and her half brother, the thirteen-year-old Carl, were dueling with hardwood practice swords. Since they now had real swords, and someone who knew how to use one, the students now included Janan and Jube.

Zackoro sat on a long-legged stool, calling instruction as they worked. Not yet able to give personal instruction, he would call them over to his stool to position their limbs, or demonstrate a movement of the weapon.

***

When the twins were old enough to do without their mother, and before the coming of Minna and Zackoro, Janan had left them with their grandparents and younger half-uncle. When it had been thoroughly explained to them, the girls thought it a hoot to have an uncle younger than themselves.

"Da, it is time, and past, that we find out what is happening in the world; I am tired of going through our old village to hunt and gather. It is dangerous. Do you know a path to the east?"

"No, girl, and I checked well over the years. The only path that comes out of the Desolation east of us begins not too far north of our village, and angles north and east to come out at the trace due east of us near where the trace meets the Plain. What keeps us safe here is that mountain barrier. There could be a way through to the other side, I suppose, so it would no' be a bad idea to check every small crack and cranny in the hills now that we have the time."

Janan sat thinking for some time, then said, "I'll do the checking, Da, if you will think up games for the twins and Carl. It is time to begin their education, and I seem to remember you starting me on weapons practice that way. Meg can start them on their letters, even if we don't have any scrolls. If I don't show up once every seven-day, you can come hunt me. I will mark my path and pull down my cairns as I come back out. I use four stones."

Janan started searching a league south of the valley, and worked her way north. She came close to a bad fall a time or two but had always made it back to the valley every seven-day. After resting a few days she continued the search. She was a league north of the valley and had found no way through the barrier that protected their hideaway.

"Guess I will have to work farther north and south," she mumbled as she chewed on a piece of jerky. Staring at a fair-sized cave entrance, she grinned. "Maybe I could go under the barrier range." She stopped grinning; a rabbit had come from the cave. With mouth hanging open, Janan watched the little animal crawl from the opening. And crawl it did; all she had to do was to walk over and pick it up.

Back in her bit of shade, Janan poured water into her cupped hand and offered it to the wiggle nose. Finally satisfied, the long ear crouched in her lap, watching her with unblinking eyes. Finally it tried, weakly, to escape, only to end up in Janan's carry sack. Tying the top closed, she said, "Well, Sir Long of Ears, time for us to go home."

Back in the valley, the delighted youngsters began the job of taming the newcomer. Green, leafy things from the garden, water in a small bowl, and a bit of salt now and again did the job. Soon Sir Long Ears was a pet, and a pest. One rabbit couldn't eat all that much, but Jube frequently swore he was going to have rabbit stew if he caught the thing in his garden just one more time.

"Da, that thing had to come from the Green Lands."

"Aye, but it could come through holes that a man could no' come through, and we don't know how long it was lost in the cave. Caves be dangerous places to be lost in, girl."

"I think, Da, with Meg's little candle lantern and with my little markers, it should not be all that bad." Her twinkling grey eyes were a-star with good humor, and as she chuckled she played with her single, thick braid of red-gold hair. "Mayhap Sir Long of Ear left a trail, and I can carry a piece of hide with me, along with pen and ink. A map of my trail, and using cairn markers, should keep me safe enough."

"While I am looking, will you see if you can figure a way to make coins out of those nuggets you found? If we can get to the trace we might waylay a trader and get some supplies, along with some news. If you can figure a way to make coins, you can put my name on one side and Antore's on the other, with a diagonal line across his name."

"I got some coin, girl, and can use them to make molds. Better yet, I can carve a couple of wood patterns and, using a sand and clay mold, pour a soft-iron double mold. I brought my arrowhead kit along, and the melt pot was too small for Meg to use. Gold will melt before soft-iron." He nodded. "I can make a good mold of iron, but why put those names on the coin?"

"If I can find a route out of the Desolation, I want to send a message to Antore."

"And if you cannot find this route of yer's?"

"Then, Da, I will have to keep using the route I have been, and maybe catch me a trader somewhere east of the village."

"This coin business sounds downright foolish to me; can't you let well enough alone? Antore is beyond reach, girl. We can use the nuggets for trading."

She had long brooded about Antore. "One day, Jube, I will toll him within reach, then I will want some gold arrowheads, with 'Janan' on them."

"Foolishness," Jube grumbled while thinking that it would be a good thing to have access to a trader or two.

Janan's deerskin map was of an extensive maze when she finally pushed through a bush hiding the opening to a fair-sized cave. The sign in the cave was fox, and the first thing she did was to mark the opening the same way animals marked their territory; besides, she needed to pee. Jube had told her, years ago, that such a marking would keep even bear out of a cave so marked.

Studying the lay of the land, she found it good. Nothing here to attract a human. The cave was in a deep depression, high in the side of the Desolation. The only thing growing here was the oilwood bush that hid the opening. The rock all around would not show track.

Janan found a good lookout, with a boulder and a bush for cover, then she settled down to watch. She had five days left before Jube would come hunting her. After a full day of spying out the land she had seen no sign of man, no smoke, no movement, no sound, just the trace where it broke out of the trees and onto the Gempore Plain to the north.

Trader Jokome was glad to be out of the trees and on the plain. King Antore had made it hot for bandits, so he had not had to fight or run for the past two years, yet it was good to be on the plain. The king was a hard dog's get, but his feud with the bandits caused the traders to support him.

Someone sitting beside the trace, leaning against a large rock, caused Jokome to rein his team to a halt and lift a crossbow to his lap, use the cocking lever, and slide home a quarrel. The figure leaning against the rock was clad in buckskins, and the only weapon showing was the spear that leaned against the same rock. The figure stood to throw the spear down behind the rock and wave in greeting.

Chucking to his team, he let them walk toward the buckskin clad…woman! Yes, it was a woman. As he again pulled his team to a halt, she called out, "Heyla, Jokome, old thief."

He scowled. No one called him a thief without coming to grief, no one! Except…who was it? Oh yes, that smart-mouthed old hunter down south. But that village had been gone for a long number of years.

The woman walked to the side of the wagon, then raised her elegant brows. "Are things so bad, Jokome, that you threaten me with a crossbow?"

She used the same jocular tone of voice as had that old hunter when he had named the very young trader "old thief." Come to think of it, the hunter had always had a young girl with him.

"No one calls me a thief!"

"It seems to me that I remember Jube calling you that while offering hospitality."

Jube! Yes, that was the name. How could he have forgotten Jube? He had been the nearest thing to a friend that Jokome had. He shook his head. "You cannot be Jube's little girl, surely."

Suddenly there was a knife at his throat and another hovering over the bow string of his crossbow. "If you will carefully remove the bolt from your bow and release the tension on the string, I will sheathe my knives."

He could feel his face turning red. Caught like a rank amateur, a seasoned trader like him. Caught by a woman! He had just two choices; he could unload the crossbow and wait for her friends to arrive, or chance getting his throat cut. He unloaded the bow, only to have a third choice dropped on him.

"Sorry about this, friend of me da, but now we are even; you have your knives and I have mine." As she said this, her knives found their holders, and she smiled at his surprise. "Now, happen we can do a little trading." Her smile grew. "And Da will be glad to hear tidings of you. More than glad, I think."

Trading! Now *that* he could understand. "What have you to trade?" He eyed her speculatively. "I see no trade goods."

She grinned, then laughed. "Not that, ye trader dog, I mis-spoke. I should have said that I want to buy some of your goods. I need some nested pots, a teapot, some soft-iron stock, clothing or cloth, lots of candles, salt, seed, and some candle lamps and lanterns."

"And what do you use to pay for these goods? I have what you want, except for the seed. What coin do you use?"

She was smiling as she flipped him a coin. "Gold, old thief."

Deftly catching the coin, he looked at it while saying, "Will you quit calling me that! And I don't recognize the coinage." He bit the coin. "What is its worth?"

"You will have to test it and scale it, and I will quit calling you that name when I see the result of your scale and your prices."

Jokome climbed down and lowered the side of the wagon to turn it into a table. Carefully he set up his scales and brought out an honest set of weights, then the girl handed him three more coins. Although none of the four coins was the same weight, there was more than enough to buy what she had mentioned.

He saw two names on the coins, but one had a line across it. Staring at the unblemished name, he said, "I don't recognize where this was coined. Whose name is this?"

"It was coined in these woods, Trader Jokome, the realm of Jube, and that name is Janan Jubedottir."

Jokome was well pleased with his sales. The woman, Janan, had bought just what she could carry in the fine pack he had sold her. She had bargained, but she was an amateur. Though she had caught him out on the tea ball that should have gone with the teapot, he had doubled his cost on the spools of thread she had bought, and more, because she had no empty spools to trade in. All in all, he had made a quarter more than the goods would have brought in the king's town. He had even tried to sell her his spare set of scales. "So you can scale your coin." He wanted the other two coins, but she decided she had all she could carry. Just as well, he had only one set of honest weights. After he had watched her walk down the trace and into the wood, he set out for his destination, frowning over the second name on the coins she had given for his goods.

Five

This was his second trip this year, and it was the second year since Jokome had first met with Jube's girl; he had often wondered about her and Jube. She was a looker, that one, in her tight buckskins; those grey eyes of hers could almost talk; and that braid was like red gold. He often thought of her low, sensuous chuckle and that flawless, golden tan, and...

He had kept watch for the woman from the moment he entered the wood, because she had hinted that they lived in the south of the wood. All his inquiries had met with failure. Some of those few living in the wood remembered Jube, but all thought him dead or gone west.

"Heyla, Jokome."

He let out a startled yelp and almost jumped out of his skin. Janan was calmly walking alongside his wagon. "Are you ready to cheat me out of some more of my gold? Jube wanted to come along with me, so he could put some knots on your head. He said you undervalued my gold and overcharged for your goods."

"Dammee, woman, do you want to give me heart-stop! Where did you drop from?"

"Oh, I was standing beside the trace when you went by, and you just ignored me, so I thought I should speak up. There are four traders already at the campsite, so I thought I better do my trading before you get there. Traders seem to be a touchy breed, and there is no safe way to come into that camp, nor do I want to spend the night there."

He frowned. "Are the four traders traveling together?"

"Aye, and from what I overheard, they think there are bandits in the wood. But not to worry, old son, there is a pair of traders behind you that you can join up with. Now, why don't you pull over so I can load my pack and be on my way."

Janan had stayed with the trader until the two following him hove into view, then she had bid him a fair journey and disappeared into the wood.

That night, with the seven wagons circled, the traders were cooking over a communal fire. The two that had arrived with Jokome were talking about the "fellow" they had seen leaving his wagon.

"Young Jokome, don't you realize how dangerous it is to stop in the middle of the wood? That one could have robbed you and cut your throat."

"Ah, friend Barazzo, she be a regular customer of mine and told of your coming, because she thought I should join with the two of you. She waited your arrival as a precaution. She is always well armed and has knowledge of arms work."

"A woman! But she wore buckskin and knives and carried a spear. I thought she was a man! Who is she?"

Jokome decided it best that he did not know her. "Don't rightly know. She buys some goods and always pays well but doesn't have a lot to say. I have heard tales of a band of woman warriors, south across the sea, but I heard they be dark of skin. This one's skin be browned by sun and wind."

This was enough to get the storytelling going. Jokome's customer was forgotten.

Janan had met the trader well south of the cave and had laid a trail toward the south until she came to the verge of the Desolation. Where she left no trail, she turned north. Now almost to the cave, she heard a woman scream. The girls! She ran toward the sound. On hearing the sound of weapon on weapon, she shed her pack and ran toward the battle sounds.

Nearest Janan was a laughing warrior. Beyond him was another, who had crossed blades with a gowned woman. The laughing warrior, said, "Come on, Jut, disarm her and let's get to it. It been so long since I been with a woman, I maybe forget what one is for."

Janan's rage was instant, and the laughing one fell forward after her spear had cut through the back of his neck and severed his spine. The sword-wielding warrior slapped the sword out of his opponent's hands, laid the flat of his blade against her head, and turned on Janan. As she yanked her spear from the neck of her victim, her new opponent pulled a long knife to make a two-bladed assault on the spear carrier.

When he parried her first assault in a way that left her no use of the butt of the spear, Janan knew she was in trouble. As he beat aside a butt attack, she drew her knife and cast it. His knife deflected it, and he moved in, swinging his sword. Her defense almost cost her the spear, then a feathered arrow appeared in his throat. The arrow had passed close enough that she felt the wind of its passing. A second arrow buried itself in his chest.

"Girls?"

"Aye."

"I thought I told you to stay in the cave and keep watch."

"We did, and a good thing, too. Watched that woman drag that funny-looking thing past, then watched the two men following her track, then we saw you turn off and go after them. That was when I decided that you might need a backup. Seems I was right, Ma."

"All right, all right! And, Deeta, your mother is proud of you; glad you two were smart enough to do the right thing. That one was damn canny and just might have taken me. Thank you, dear."

Her daughter walked up, and Janan put an arm around her. "Where is Lee?"

"Right here, Ma. I was backing Dee."

Janan chuckled. "All right, let's see about the lady."

The "lady" had a bruise on her jaw and was trying to come around. The application of a wet cloth on her bruise woke her, and a drink of cool water cleared her eyes.

Leeta had been prowling the area, an arrow ready, looking for trouble. Dee's arrow had been first, and Lee just knew she would put on airs.

"Ma, there is another man over here."

Dee came to her feet and snatched up her bow.

"No, no, don't hurt him!" The injured woman struggled to rise.

Holding her down, Janan said, "What is he doing?"

"Just lying here, Ma. He is breathing, but that is all he is doing. He is all rolled up in a blanket and is lying on that contraption she was pulling."

"Please, he is wounded and needs help."

Janan sighed and said, "Another one of Antore's cast-asides?"

"How did you know?"

"I know Antore. How did you get mixed up in this?"

"Antore was in the field, watching his army run down a bandit band. Zackoro is an army officer and was wounded by a chance arrow. They took his horse and just left him for dead. When it got dark I went back for him and got him into the woods, but I was missed and they came looking for me."

Janan nodded slowly. "I suppose he still uses that be-damned eunuch?"

She hung her head. "How did you know?" she again asked.

"I was in the same fix a few years back. I wish I had known he was in the field. I might have been able to put an arrow into his black heart. How was it that you and this Zacko—whatever—came to know each other? Oh, never mind, let's get things organized. Lee, you go get some ropes ready and pick up my pack on your way. Dee, you make a bundle of all the extra blades."

She turned to the woman they had rescued. "You…aah…" As she hesitated, the woman supplied her name. Minna. "All right, Minna, let's see to your man."

Minna's man was fevered, but he did not seem to have a wound sickness. The arrow seemed to have missed the vitals; then Janan found the broken leg. When the arrow had taken him, he had fallen from his horse, breaking the big bone of the upper leg. Janan did not have a lot in her medicine kit, but she went to work anyway. She dosed Zacko-whatever for the fever, then poulticed the arrow wound and re-wrapped it. He passed out completely when she straightened his leg, so she went the whole way.

"Dee, you help Minna hold him by the shoulders while I pull on his leg." She felt, more than saw, the ends of the break come together. Making a twisting splint and getting rid of the bodies took a lot of time, so it was near dark when they gathered in the cave.

With the help of ropes and the two girls, Janan had dragged the stretcher they had made up to the cave. Again with the help of the girls, the bodies were dragged down to the trace, where they were hung from a tree limb that overhung the trace. Janan then strung a strip of deerskin between the bodies. The message written on the deerskin was, "DOG ANTORE—NEXT TIME YOU COME—JANAN." On the way back they wiped out all signs and used brooms to insure there was no sign of their passage up the rock.

"Lee, take my pack and go get Jube and Meg. Tell Meg what we have on our hands, and tell Da we will meet them in the cathedral."

When the light from Leeta's candle lantern had gone, Janan said, "Ladies, there is no rest for the wicked. Deeta, put everything back in the slit, then you handle the extra blades and my spear. Minna and I will take the man and will go first."

When Dee climbed back down from the high crack in the rock, where extra equipment was hidden, Janan told her, "Make sure that there is nothing left to show anyone has ever been here, and scatter the animal bones around so it will look like this may be the den of a big cat. Let's go, girls. It will be a long, hard night. Dee, watch that we don't leave signs of our passage, and don't forget to pee before you leave."

The cathedral was a big, roomy cave opening, with a single large stalactite nearly meeting an equally large stalagmite. A pool of water that had been formed by the cause of the large decorations was a welcome that was found halfway through the underside of the rugged mountain range.

Meg had dosed the patient with something that left him senseless while she worked on his leg. She had removed the splint Janan had put on the leg, and had worked the bone until she was satisfied. She then wrapped the leg in cloth and sticks. Mixing a special fast-drying clay, she plastered the leg from hip to ankle, with little holes all through the clay.

"What be the holes for, old girl?" Jube and Jan were helping with the plaster work.

"Air holes, old goat. The leg must have air. That leg will be itching enough without a lot of sweat to make more itching. Now shut your yap and make me some tea. I'm in need."

The old folk had left a disgruntled Lee with her younger uncle, Carl, to watch over the valley, and had brought wood, medical supplies and food.

"When this clay is dry we will be able to move him to the valley without causing more damage." Meg grinned. "When he wakes up, I have a pain killer that won't knock him out, but the leg itch may make him wish I would."

While waiting for the clay to dry they were eating a meal, and Janan was talking with Minna. "Now, from what you told me, it seems that you two were doing the impossible, getting together without that be-damned eunuch finding it out. How did you manage that?"

Minna smiled sheepishly. "No, we had never even spoken, but every time we saw each other our eyes would meet. I may be wrong, but I think he loves me as much as I love him."

Janan frowned. "That is crazy. Without ever talking to the man you left out in the middle of the night and tried to save him. You might have known Antore would have his men out looking for you."

"Where am I?" The voice was muzzy and rusty.

Minna took the patient's hand. "Zackoro, you are safe and a healer is seeing to you. Are you in pain?"

He blinked his eyes as if trying to clear a fuzzy mind. "Minna?"

"Yes."

"I thought I dreamed. You came, you bandaged me and carried me away. You told me that you loved me. I thought I dreamed, because I have loved you for so long. I will kill Antore and take you away."

Meg leaned over and wiped away the big drops of sweat forming on his forehead. "No need of that, lad. The two of you are already away from Antore. Now, are you in pain?"

"Aye, my leg. My chest. My head."

"Here you go, laddie, some tea. It will help. Drink it right down, because it is bitter."

Six

"Megan, I have taken your bed while you sleep on the floor. I am able to sleep on the floor now, so you can have your bed back."

"Not to worry, Zack. I will soon have my bed back. Jube and the kids have almost finished your hut. Min, stop rubbing that leg and start bending it, hip and knee. We must stretch and get some strength in those muscles. This afternoon we will take him out in the sun, but not long enough to burn him. Zack, when you have had your sun, work your good leg and your arms with the weights. When you are nice and tired, try to move your gimpy leg. Min, pull that cover over his other two legs and keep working his bad leg."

Minna blushed and adjusted the cover before working his left leg.

Meg grinned, then said, "You will be living alone, Zacko, me boy. Min will still be staying with Janan in her hut."

"But why, Meg? We have planned to move into our own hut."

"Oh no, lad, there will be none of that. Had the rooms we built on to Jan's hut for the kids been big enough, you could have slept in the boy's room, and Minna in with the girls. Then Jube's and my old bones would have been a lot happier. With you in your own hut, everyone will be happy."

"I won't!"

"Now, now, Zackoro, don't get excited. I would not let Jube in my bed until he said the words, and I will not let you and Min live alone unless you have done the same."

"What foolishness is this? What words?"

"Words that will make you two man and wife. We may live like barbarians, but we will observe the proper ritual. I will not have you teaching the kids evil things."

He took Minna's hand. "Is this what you wish?"

She hung her head, then nodded.

"Then this we will do."

Megan's face lit up like one of her candle lamps. "It will be like old times. We will have the word taking, then a party. I don't think Jube has finished up all the wine Jan got from that trader man. In the evening we will escort you to your new home, where you will light the first fire in your new fireplace."

The sun was down, and Janan and Minna were enjoying the cool of the evening, sitting near the spring. The new hut was finished, and firewood was laid in the new fireplace.

"Tomorrow you and Zackoro will move into your new home, Min. Are you looking forward to it?"

"Oh, yes. It is like a dream come true. I do not know how Zackoro can love me, knowing that…that…well, what I was before."

"Not by choice, girl, but you are better off than I was. At least you do not carry the beast's whelp. Any children will be yours and Zackoro's."

"Oh, Jan, I am so happy it scares me. What if *he* should find us?"

"I have been to the cave, several times, and I think he has given up the search. I was there when they found our cave, but the bones scared them off. From what they said, some of them walked into one cave and found it occupied by a big cat with two kits. One look at the bones in our cave and they left in a hurry. We will give it a year, then I will seek out a trader friend and get the news."

On his twice-yearly trek to and from the king's town, Jokome met with the woman along the way, usually in the deep wood where she lived. She never showed up in the same place, and usually only in the southern woods, but it had been more than a year since they had met. The king had half his army out looking for her after a group of traders had found two of his warriors hanging from a tree. One of the traders had told Jokome about the words on the deer skin. This trip, again, she met him in the south part of the wood, and Jube was with her. And good it was to greet him. While Jokome made tea the woman slipped back into the wood.

"Jube, glad I am to see you. Now we can catch up on the happenings. I was afraid you had been killed off when your village was overrun."

"Na, na, old thief. All I got was this game leg. The one who stuck me was the one who was killed."

"Eh, I knew that gal had to be yours when she named me 'old thief.' Though, when she found I was honest, she quit using it. Said she would leave the name for your use."

"She should have still used it. I usually stay deep in the wood because of this gimp of mine, but I figgered to come this time to ask you why you cheat my girl. Your father was an honest man; surely he taught you better. I think you were too young when he let you take over his northern trade route."

"Na, na, old friend. Long years has it been since we have traded. Prices go up, and then King Antore's tax share cuts into my profits."

"King, my gimpy left hind leg, that illegitimate son of a dog is the reason for my gimp and for our village being gone. And Janan has a special crow to pick with him."

"I gathered that from all that excitement a while back. A friend told me about the message she left for him, and that reminds me of something I have always wondered about. How is it that most in your small village can read and write? Most lesser folk don't know their letters."

"Ah, Little Jo, that be a tale all its own. A well-dressed woman came to our village. It was in the days when my mother's mother was a girl, and no one ever learned where she came from. She took a husband from among the men of the village, and when her babies were old enough, she taught them their letters. As my mother told it to me, the other children thought it a good game to learn with that woman's children. By the time my mother was old enough to marry, it was a village tradition that all childings learn their letters."

Jokome's expression was thoughtful. "A high-bred woman just walks in among you, and no one comes looking for her. Strange."

Jube slowly nodded his head. "According to the old stories, she never told anyone her history."

"Nobody up the trace, Gramps."

The trader almost dropped the tea pot, and came near to putting a crick in his neck, "Dammee, don't sneak up on me like that!" The girl wore a grin, buckskins, a knife, and a light sword. She held a bow in her left hand and, along with a bright yellow blond braid, a full quiver hung down her back.

When Jube nodded his head she slipped back into the wood, and Jokome took tea to settle his nerves before saying, "Jube, do all your women move like a cat?"

"Nobody down the trace, Grampa." The trader frowned at the girl. She now had her bow hanging from one shoulder. "Can I get my new knife now, Grampa?"

"No, you don't, Dee. I get first choice." Jokome was seeing double.

"All right, girls, that is enough." The woman was back. Other than the bow the girls carried, and the red-gold braid of hair, the woman was armed and dressed like the girls. "Both of you make another wide swing. By the time you get back we will have our trading over with, and Trader Jokome will have his selection of knives laid out."

"All right, Ma. Will a quarter league do?"

"Yes, now be on your way."

"I thought I must be having eye trouble; how do you tell them apart?"

Janan smiled when Jube chuckled and said, "Kinda hard till they open their mouth. Now then, I guess we better get to our trading; those two can cover a quarter league in a hurry. You got that list, Jan?"

The packs were full when the twins returned, and they were soon in a squabble. Both wanted one of the knives displayed. The trader sighed, then dug out a duplicate and his engraving tools. When he had finished, he said, "You will need to mark your own sheath."

41

Jokome, watching them gloating over their new acquisitions, shook his head. They were making over the mayhem like maids with a new necklace.

"Jube, I wish you would change your gold coin. I don't dare use them in the king's town, and there have been times when I could have used the purchase power of that gold."

"What be the problem?"

"I somehow let one of them out, and one of the king's men found it in the tax collector's horde. There have been questions, and I must keep your coin in a special hideaway hole"

Janan's eyes narrowed. "I would much rather you put out as many as you can."

"Oh no, woman! It would be worth my life to be found with them. That is why I am glad you met me on my way south. Some of your coins may make their way back north, but not by my hand."

Janan chuckled. "So Antore is getting a little goosey, is he? Good!" Her next chuckle ran a chill down his spine. "Very well, my friend. We don't want to get you in trouble. We will make some blank coin, or carry some nuggets. Any change can be in silver coin. If we catch you heading north, we will use those. If you go south, we will use the old coin, hoping they will find their way back up to that town."

Jube and Janan were resting in the cathedral. He had overworked his leg. "This gimp is getting better, girl. Even a year ago I would not have made this trip. All this training has done me good, and the girls are getting better…no, hades take it, they are getting down right good. Carl has passed them."

Janan chuckled, then added a grin and said, "Yes, and that has them climbing the wall. They can no longer tease their child uncle. He is bigger and stronger, so they have to be quicker with sword and spear just to stay with him."

"Aye, but they better him with the bow, and that gives him his own wall to climb."

"I suppose these are good things, Da. The day is dangerous, and times to come look no better."

"Well, Jan, your two gimps are getting stronger each day. You are a match for any warrior, and the twins and Carl may be catching up with you. Old Meg is right handy with a bow, and Min is young enough to learn; that is, if Zack doesn't keep her preggers all the time."

"That calls something to mind, Da. The kids were deep in a discussion the other night and didn't notice when I came upon them. Carl was talking of trying to find our people so he could steal a wife. The twins thought buying husbands from Jokome might be a better way to go. Carl snorted at the idea and said they would have to find a man they wanted, then rope and tie him and drag him home." Janan's voice lost some of its humor. "And Lee thought they should find one for me."

"Aye, their education is lacking. Can you imagine the look on Jokome's face, 'Trader, how many gold pieces for a husband?' We give him too many surprises as it is."

Janan was wiping laugh tears from her eyes when she regained control and said, "Da, you told me you knew his father. You are not that old, are you?"

"Knew his ma, too. We were young together. They were just a bit older than me and your ma, but not by much."

"But Jokome is old. Maybe not as old as you, but old."

"Na, na, daughter, he not old. Let me recall how it was." Jube drew a stick from the fire to light his pipe. Thanks to the trader, Jube now had pipe weed growing in his garden. He leaned back, puffing contentedly. "Old Ando and me lost our wives the same year. 'Twas the pox that took them. Both of us had a young one to raise, but we couldn't get over our loss, so we never took another woman."

"As far as I know, Ando is still running his southern trade route. He gave Jokome the northern route and set him up with a wagon and goods. As he made money, Little Jo paid for the goods. The wagon, horses and fixings were his legacy."

"Little Jo?"

"It was what we called Jokome."

"Well, Little Jo looks old to me."

Jube chuckled. "He were young to be a trader, so he made up to look older." Jube tamped his pipe and relit it, then chuckled again. "Let me

43

see now…you were about ten, maybe a bit older, when he first came to the village. In that day we were the most northern part of his route. Since I knew his da, I always offered hospitality. He were about fifteen, maybe sixteen, but tried to make out that he was twice that age. He was tall, so he stooped. He were young and fair, so he wore old man clothing and scowled a lot. He even tried to make his voice old." Jube grinned and tamped his pipe with a horny finger. "That be when I began calling him 'old thief.' Guess it got to be a habit, because he still do all that. Well, he don't stoop no more."

"All right, girls, did you get your ears full?"

"Aw, how did you hear us, Ma?"

"Good ears, and you didn't put your light out soon enough. Did you see anything from the cave, and did you make sure you left no sign in the cave?"

"Yes, Ma, there was nothing as far as the eye could see, and Jokome was long gone." Dee grinned. "And we heard enough to know the trader isn't as old as we thought. Maybe one of us could get him for a husband."

"Maybe you could, girl, if you want a husband older than yer mother."

"Nooo…oh, I guess I will let Lee have him, Grandpa."

"Not me! Maybe he would do for Ma."

Janan laughed and said, "Maybe Ma doesn't want a husband, and there is always the chance Jokome doesn't want a wife, Lee."

"That doesn't matter. We just wrap him up and haul him off to the valley, and Megan can say the words over him."

"Daughter, yer daughters ain't had no proper upbringin'. If we still had our village they would know better."

Seven

"Now, girls, I think it is time, and past time, that you learn how civilized folk live and act." Janan frowned at the twins. "We are going to build something like a town plaza. This is a place where town gatherings are held, where you and Carl will learn how folk interact with one another."

She had enlisted the aid of Minna and Megan, and they and the twins were seated by the fire in Janan's hut. Meanwhile, Jube and Zackoro were talking with Carl in Jube's hut.

Minna held her and Zack's son, the year-old Erick. "I know that your mother explained how we got Erick, and you watched him being born, so we need not explain the facts of living to you. You also know that Carl is a half brother to your mother. This being true, you also know why you cannot bear his children."

Both girls nodded, then their mother said, "But you don't seem to understand how a man and woman become husband and wife."

"Sure we do, Ma," Leeta exclaimed. "Just like Meg got Grandpa, and like Min got Zack."

"Oh? And how was that?"

"Well, Ma, Meg told how she dragged Gramps off to her cave, and we saw how Min dragged Zack off to the woods."

Putting her oar in, Deeta said, "But I can't see the good in sticking a man before hauling him off. I would just lasso him, hogtie him, then march him home. No need of carrying him all that way. Why else were we taught how to make and use a lariat?"

Megan laughed until the tears came. Wiping her eyes, she shook her head, gave a weak giggle, then said, "Girls, you have just half the story. When I found your grandpa wounded, I took him to the cave to hide both him and me from Antore's men, and to heal him. When we made our way to this valley I came to think a lot of the old goat, but I wouldn't bed him until he asked me to be his wife and we said the words."

Minna smiled and, nodding her head, said, "You know how Zackoro and I came to be here, but you didn't hear him ask me to be his wife. You did, though, listen to the word taking by the two of us, and you were at the celebration."

"You mean we gotta wait for some man to ask us!" Lee was indignant. "Maybe I will just forget this husband thing!"

"I'm afraid so, Leeta." Janan's smile was just a little sad. "Normally you would have the boys in your village, and visitors from other villages, to pick from. Boys and girls normally do a lot of flirting and looking before they choose."

"What's flirting, Ma?"

"Well, Deeta, it is a lot of things. When you reach an age where boys start to mean something more than playmates to you, they will start looking at you in a different way. There will be a lot of teasing and smiling, and a bit of kiss-stealing by the boys at the village dances and celebrations. Sometimes the girl will act indignant, even when she is really pleased. Eventually the right one will ask you to marry him and, if the two families agree, the boy builds a house. At the word-taking celebration, family and friends make gifts of the things needed to make a house a home. At the end of the celebration the new husband and wife are escorted to their new home, where the wife lights the first fire in their fireplace. Everyone then wishes them well and leaves them in peace, as we did with Zackoro and Minna."

"Well, if I can't lasso the one I pick out, I won't wait for him to ask me, I'll just ask him. But it sounds like a lot of nonsense to me."

"No, Lee, it is a lot of fun, and rather wonderful."

Dee was wide-eyed. "Did you do any of that, Ma?"

Janan's smile was sad. "Oh, yes. But the war ruined all that when our village was overrun."

Lee had a big grin. "Is that how you got Antore, Ma?" She knew she had said something wrong when there came a strained quiet around the fire; the only sound was of logs shifting in the fireplace.

Finally Megan broke the silence. "No, girls, Antore broke all the laws. He stole your mother from her home, and he held her prisoner for two years. A king Antore may be, but his life is forfeit to any of the family that can reach him."

Dee frowned. "But…aren't we Antoredottir?"

Janan put one arm around each of her daughters and said, "No! You are mine. My strong, lovely, bullheaded Janandottir."

The next day Carl and the girls wandered out to the pasture. Their elders watched them go and, understanding the youngsters need to discuss the new information, left them in peace.

In the shade of a tree near the valley wall there were rocks to sit on while they shared the information from the two meetings of the night before. Carl had not received the flirting story, just the part about the asking, the need to get the families permission, and, of course, the word-taking and celebration.

Being a serious young man, Carl thought about what the girls told him and came to the conclusion that they should ask the "old folk" to show them how all this was done.

"Then I will go to the village, and from there I will travel west. Da has told me of the villagers escaping in that direction. Maybe I can find them."

Lee brightened and said, "Aye, and we will go with you. Sounds like fun."

Megan had a small shepherd's pipe and Jube a drum. In the past they had helped with music for the village celebrations. Jube used a single two-headed drumstick, bringing forth a surprisingly intricate patter from his small drum. To the beat of the drum Megan taught the steps for individual, pairs and group dancing to the youngsters and to Min and

Zack. The latter pair knew some of the village steps and added some from their home villages.

Then, with Jube and Meg providing the music, the younger six danced and sang the old songs. With the singing and dancing, storytelling, jokes and village history, they tried to recreate the nighttime activities of a typical village plaza.

These activities kept the group entertained each night for nearly two moons. The twins learned to pipe and drum, allowing Meg and Jube to join in the festivities. The twins' music was a bit shaky, but it served. Some nights the dancing was disrupted by laughter when the simulated flirting became so outrageous that all were helpless with laughter. Then Carl became restless.

One night, seated around the fire pit in the center of their "plaza," they listened to Jube's tale. He had just finished a tale from his boyhood, when he had traveled far to the south to see the big water and the strange people who sailed into the ports there.

The words Carl dropped into the quiet following Jube's story was like a splash of cold water. "Da, I have decided to do some hunting westward. I go to find our village, those who fled west from the village."

Jube frowned and moved his head a little, from side to side. "No, too dangerous for one lad alone."

"He wouldn't be alone, Gramps. Dee and I will be with him."

Again Jube made the slight negative movement of his head. "Nay, that would be worse. The two of you being with him would make the danger worse by ten times. Besides, how would you know when you found them? None of you would know a villager from a bandit."

He held up a hand, quelling Lee's instant outrage. "I have been thinking about this very thing ever since we be dancing and carrying on." Again his upheld hand quieted the three. "I be thinking of going meself, but—" He turned to look at Megan. "What you do you think about it, old girl?"

Megan sat in thought for a time, then said, "You were right sprightly in the dancing, and you do all right on your visits to the trader." She imitated his slight head shake. "But for a long haul, I don't know. Face it, old man, we have a lot of years on us, and your leg is not as strong as it could be."

"I hate to admit it, Meg, but you may be spoutin' the truth. I could hold me own in battle, but for a long walk…" He shook his head. "Still, I would like to know about our folk. We could ask Zack to go with Carl, but he would be a stranger too."

"Grandpa, couldn't you tell us what to look for. Carl is a man, and me and Dee can fight like a man. With the three of us armed to the teeth nobody would bother us."

Janan had held her peace, listening and thinking. "I don't think so, Leeta. One of those going would need to be of the village, and that means Megan, Da or me."

"What be in yer thinking, girl?"

"That you are right, Da. It would be a good thing to find our people. If they are well situated, and not too far away, we might want to join them. We could move slow and take our stock. Maybe we could buy a wagon and team." Now Janan imitated her father's small head shake. "But we can't plan anything until we know we can find them and know that we want to join them."

"Then you can go with us, Ma. That way we would have four to do the fighting."

"Lee, you and Dee are not going!"

"Aw, Ma!"

"No! You don't know what you are asking. Zack or I should be here, and I don't think we want to remove four of our best fighters from our defenses. We have never had to worry, but that could change."

"But there is nothing to do except practice, and I am tired of that."

"Well, Leeta," Janan's smile was a bit grim, "that is what we will all be doing until this is well thought out. Meantime, I think we will work out some escape routes. Da, didn't you tell me of a route that came out in the middle of the wildwood? After that I think we should investigate that little cave where your grandpa finds those little nuggets. The gravel where he finds those nuggets shows that water used to come out of that cave. If that little cave should happen to connect with our cave labyrinth, it would give us a good retreat. Should we ever get trapped in this little green hole in the ground, the caves just might be the saving of us."

The planning and small cave held their interest for seven days, but all the side passages in the cave petered out until Carl and the girls found a large opening that ended in a deep pit.

Carl found a rock and tossed it into the pit. After a long wait, Dee whispered, "Maybe it doesn't have a bottom," and backed away from the lip of the hole just as the sound of a splash echoed up the walls of the deep opening.

Then Lee backed away, "We better go get Gramps."

Carl watched the twins go, then walked a few feet in their wake, only to stop at an opening to his right, "Dumb girls didn't even look at this one," he mumbled as he shined his lantern down a narrow passageway.

When Jube and Janan came to see the wonder, Lee tossed a large rock into the hole. It was a long count before they heard it hit water. Then Janan lay on the stone floor, her head over the edge of the pit, saying, "Everyone be quiet!"

After she had listened intently for a time, Janan stood to brush off her clothing, "There is a lot of running water down there, and there is a small stream running down the other side of this hole. I would guess the stream that used to run out of this cave into our valley was undercut by a bigger stream." She turned to her father. "Da, this may be where that waterfall comes from. It just comes out of a bluff and falls over a low cliff."

"Could be, girl, and I guess this ends your search for a getaway hole?"

No one had missed Carl until his voice echoed from behind them, "Don't neither!" Carl was grinning. "Those dumb girls saw the big opening and walked right by a little one. While they went for you two I checked it out; it doesn't stay little very long, and it may hook up with the other caves." Both girls were showing him the tip of their tongue.

It took two seven-days, but they finally added a new branch to their cave complex. All this had given Janan time to think.

Janan's decision outraged the twins. Carl and their mother would be going to hunt for the village folk. Carl could go, but the twins had to stay with Zack, Minna and the old folk.

None of the twins' arguments swayed their mother as preparations were made for the trip. Carl's sly comments did little to cool the temper of the two.

When Janan and Carl had gone, the twins sulked until their grandfather told them to make a list of things needed from the trader. "'Bout time for Jokome to be passing by on his way to Dog Town." For Jube it was never the king's town or, as it was coming to be called, Kingston.

About the time Janan and her half brother finished scouting around the village site and headed west, the twins and Jube used the new branch of their labyrinth to start on their trip to meet the trader.

Eight

Janan and Carl's track was like a snake's trail through the wildwood. As they worked their way west they wandered toward the southwest, then to the northwest and back again; they looked for a sign anyone had passed that way. They stopped early each evening to make a fire and cook whatever game they could take. Fruit and roots were to be found, so they ate pretty well and saved their trail stew makings.

"I doubt we find any sign of their passing, Carl." They were eight days on their journey, and had found no sign that man had touched the wildwood. "It has been just too many years since their trek, and it is obvious that no one even hunts here."

"So how long will we keep on heading west?"

Janan smiled. "Until we find them or get tired of walking. What say you to one moon?"

Carl just nodded, then said, "I need to find a bush," and walked off into the wood. The stew was ready, and the water for tea was boiling when he returned.

"Better come take a look, Jan. I found something."

The name carved into the rock of the crude headstone read, "Hober Anselsson."

Janan made the cross sign, then said, "Aye, even when I was little, Hober was an old gray head. When the village folk were leaving I saw his son loading him into a horse cart. Guess the excitement was too much for him. A shame, really. I can still remember the stories he told when I was a lass. Well, brother, looks like we are on the right track. Come on, let's get back to the fire before the tea water boils away."

The next morning, while Carl made up their packs, Janan carried a handful of wildflowers to the grave. Leaning them against the headstone, she said, "Sleep well, elder."

Carl was burying the remains of their fire when she returned. Taking up her pack, she turned and looked north, checking the distance to the Desolation. "It looks like they headed due west, Carl."

Jokome found Jube and the twins waiting at the trader's campsite. "Heyla, Jube, how is it your girl let you come without her along to look after you?"

"Hey, old thief, are you lookin' for a knot on yer hard head?"

The twins grinned when the trader said, "At least she sent the girls to see that you don't get in any trouble." He climbed down from the wagon and stretched. "Ah, that's better, Jube. I have to drive straight through from Picket Town now, and I get stiff between stops. When your old town was still around I could lay up there, then head back south. Now I have to make two stops in the wood before this one. I usually don't use this camp unless I am headed south. Going north, and I get here this early, I go on to the camp on the plain."

Jube nodded. "Us were your turn around, before. Now I guess you got no towns between Picket and Dog Town. How many stops on the plain before you get to that place? Even before Antore, I never used the plain any, and that town was just a den of thieves."

"Really not that far after I hit the plain. It's just about half a day from the wood to the campsite, about the same from the camp to Kingston. As for the town, after Antore and his army cleaned it out, it got to be a fair place to do business."

"Kingston? Hey, they change the name?"

Jokome shrugged and grinned before saying, "Easy to say. Guess the town folk decided to shorten it some."

Jube nodded, saying, "Well, you ought to have company; three traders passed by about two hours ahead of you." Turning to the twins, he growled, "Haven't you got that fire lit yet? Get on it! I'm hungry!" He grinned at the trader. "You got the pot, we got the fixin's for a good old-fashioned village stew, with fresh vegetables, fresh meat and all. Old Meg had the teachin' of these two, and they do 'bout as good as she does. We can get our tradin' done while they cook."

Later, as the girls cleaned up the bowls, cups and pot, they were grumbling at the men. Lee was in particular. "We did the cooking; couldn't you at least help with the clean-up?"

Jokome patted his stomach and said, "Ladies, you have no one to blame but yourselves. That is the finest meal I have eaten since I left home. I am so stuffed, and I couldn't bend over to help you."

Dee finished re-packing Jokome's bowls, then asked, "Your wife cook this kind of stew?"

Jokome chuckled and shook his head. "No, I do. Not having a wife, I do my own cooking, but you do better than I can at stew making. I do bake a mean pone of bread, though, and I can make good wheat bread."

When Dee mumbled that she had never heard of wheat bread, he promised to bring the makings for a loaf his next trip north.

Jube had his pipe fired up, so Jokome pulled his old black hat off and fired up his own. While he and Jube talked about the old days, he noticed the girls staring at him and whispering. Finally he looked directly at the pair, and frowned. "What's the matter, girls?" He smoothed his long, dark brown beard. "Did I leave food in my beard?"

What the twins had been seeing was a man without his habitual frown and, for the first time, without his hat on his head. Neither the shoulder-length wavy hair, the color of the beard, nor the long beard had any silver mixed with the brown.

Caught off guard, Dee lost all discretion. "No, but why do you wear that old black clothing and that dirty old hat?"

Lee grew a big grin. "And why don't you trim up that old beard of yours and that wild hair? Washed up, trimmed up, and with set of good clothing, I bet you'd look downright pretty."

The expression on Jokome's red face caused Jube to laugh till he hurt. Finally getting his breath, Jube was still chuckling when he said, "Well, old thief?"

Dee was grumpy. "We heard Grandpa telling Ma about when you first started trading, but you're no boy now. You got no reason to keep dressing like an old man."

With a huge frown on his face, Jokome jammed his hat on his head and said, "I have other clothing, but these are my trading duds." Coming to his feet, he knocked the dottle out of his pipe, looked at the sun and said, "Well, Jube, I guess I'll be on my way. I want to make the plains camp by dark. I don't like to camp anymore than I have to in the wood. Up there the horses can get some rest and some grazing. I figure to be in town for about a moon. Will I be seeing you on my way back?"

"Don't know, Little Jo, my boy and Janan have gone west lookin' for our village folk. If they are gone too long I may have to take a little walk and look for them."

"That is wooly country, Jube. I don't think you should have let her go." Jube wondered at his expression, but it was there and gone again. Turning to the girls, the trader frowned and said, "As for you two, despite your bad manners, I thank you for the meal." He climbed up to the seat of his wagon, then looked down at the grinning pair and chucked to his horses. As the wagon moved off, he turned back to them. "And, for your information, I don't think I will *ever* be pretty."

When they arrived back in the valley, the three wayfarers were tired. While they rested, Meg and Min unpacked what Jube and the twins had carried home. Over the evening meal, Jube told of their trip.

When the tale came to where the twins had ganged up on Jokome, Meg was chuckling. Min was laughing outright when Megan tried to assume a severe expression. "Here we have been trying to civilize you two hellions, and what do you do? You up and insult an older man."

It was the irrepressible Lee who answered the accusation. "Na, he is not old. And the way he dresses, along with that hair and beard of his, now *that* is the insult."

"It doesn't look like our Desolation." Carl and Janan stood looking at the dry country blocking their way.

Janan grunted her agreement. "Dry sand and a lot more bush." She looked both ways. "Now we have to figure out if they went south or straight on through it."

Carl nodded, then eyed the hills to the north of them. "Maybe we could climb high enough to see how far this sand stretches to the south."

Janan just nodded before heading toward the hill that was the farthest out in the sand. Arriving at the westernmost spur of the hills, she slid out of her pack with a sigh. "Light a spell, Carl, and I will see what can be seen."

The climb wasn't bad, and the lookout peak was adequate for a good look south. There seemed no end to the sand, north or south. When she returned from the heights, Carl was missing, but the packs were still there. Lifting her water skin from where it lay by the packs, Janan wet her whistle and then used it.

After a while Carl came trudging through the sand from around the end of the spur. Throwing a thumb over his shoulder, he said, "Cave back that way. No animal sign, but I think I found a fire pit; it was too dim to be sure."

Janan, raising both brows, said, "All right, let's load up and go have a look."

Arriving at the entrance to the cave, they again slipped out of their packs, and Janan dug out the candle lantern she had brought along. The entrance to the cave was wide enough for three to walk abreast, and tall enough that they did not have to bend over. It was just one big room with no other exits.

"Here, Jan, right in the middle." The light showed them a circle of stone almost covered with sand. When Carl dug in the middle of the circle he turned up charcoal. On the right wall they found scratches of ill-defined letters.

"This one," Janan pointed to a set of letters at about the height of her waist, "looks to spell 'Derek' and that is about the right height for the one I remember. Up here is 'Anna,' his older sister. There is still some smoke sign on the ceiling, so they must have stayed a while." She shrugged, "Now if we can just figure out where they went from here." She sighed before adding, "I'm tired, Carl, and I think it wouldn't hurt if we were to lay over for a couple days' rest."

"I won't give you an argument, Jan. I'll go rustle up some firewood."

"I'll go with you. Let's get our gear in here, then try to bring in enough wood for a couple of days anyway." She walked to the cave entrance and checked the sky. "Looks like we are due for some wet weather, and I would rather rest dry than march wet. Let's get in enough wood for several days."

Zack came trudging up to the entrance to the valley, carrying a green hide full of deer meat, and whistled the signal. Before long someone pulled the gate out of the way, and Zack bent low to make his way through the prickly tunnel.

After Zackoro passed her, Megan looked back through the tunnel. "Where's Jube?"

"He decided to trail Janan and Carl a little way, then come on back. He wanted to be sure they were well on their way."

"That old fool is trying to get himself killed, and I am already having second thoughts about letting Carl and Jan go off like that. Why didn't you go with him?"

"We already had the meat, and Jube didn't want it to spoil. Said he was a hunter and didn't need a soldier-boy getting in his way. That was all right with me. Now we need to get right on this meat and the hide. Had a good moon, so I just kept walking. Still, the meat will get high if we don't get it worked up right away."

"Right. Min and I will go to work on it while you get a nap. When you come alive, you can help. That stone smoker you made should take it all."

The smoker was already going by the time Zack "came alive" and went to the spring to wash his face and comb his hair. The two women chuckled when he checked to be sure they didn't have too much fire in the smoker.

Meg grinned. "What's the matter, Zack? Think we don't know how to smoke meat?"

His return smile was just a shade sheepish, so he turned his back on them and had a good stretch while he looked around the quiet valley. Too quiet! Turning back to the women, he said, "Where are the girls?"

"They went to check the cave opening." Meg shrugged. "They said they might do a little hunting if it was quiet."

Zackoro was frowning when he said, "And now I don't like it, Meg. We are too scattered, what with two gone west, Jube nosing around on their trail, us here, and those two young hellions hunting near the plain. Maybe I should go check on the girls."

Again Meg shrugged. "They are about grown, Zack, and you yourself said they could fight like a man. Give them a day to get there, a day to hunt, and a day to get back, then you can start worrying."

Nine

Seated on his throne, King Antore was listening to his elderly chamberlain. "Sire, the traders, those that will admit having them, say all of those gold coins now come from the deep south. I would say the makers of the coin have turned tail and have fled your realm."

Resting an elbow on his knee, Antore rested his chin in the palm of his hand. Frowning, he said, "And I am not yet strong enough to demand anything from that southern kingdom. Too bad, I would have liked to get my hands on that witch. First she kills two of my men, leaving an insulting message, then these coins." He looked at the coin in his hand. "Janan," he growled.

The hair beneath the simple gold crown was just beginning to silver and, despite the weapon master's best efforts, Antore's body was showing the effects of too much good food and wine, and not enough exercise.

He shrugged. "Well, we will keep an eye open for any woman wearing buckskins and weapons. One of the traders told of a woman seen in the wood well south who dressed like that." He shrugged again. "Perhaps we should give it up, but that witch was picked up down that way." He chuckled. "And she knew how to use a weapon. She even tried to use my own knife on me." Antore shook his head. "She was a little bit of a thing, and pretty as a picture; I wonder how she turned out."

Janan was studying the cave writings when she found another clue. "Come look at this, Carl." What Carl saw as Janan walked her lantern down a three-arm-length pictorial looked to be a map.

"There are X marks in five places, with three wavy lines below each. Janan looked closer. "But what are these vertical lines above the marks? The marks probably show camping places. If the wavy lines mean water that would make sense, but the vertical lines…I don't know!"

Carl studied the scratch marks with a frown on his face. Then the frown went away. With his usual brevity he said, "Trees."

Janan stared at the marks intently, then grinned. "You know, I think you are right. Look at the far left end. There are a whole lot of those upright marks and an arm-length of those wavy lines. It is a wood and a stream, or a river. Well, brother, I think I can guess at where our folk ended up. Feel up to a long walk in the sand?"

He grunted, then said, "We better load up on water and what extra food we can carry. When we find that first water hole we will have some idea how far it is across this Desolation."

The five days of rest had helped, and the buck Carl had brought down had fed them and furnished smoked meat to add to their store. Janan had found and gathered enough reeds to make a couple of sun hats. Both checked their trail gear and weapons. Both carried a pair of knives, a sword and a bow. Both quivers were full, and Janan carried a bundle of extra arrows strapped to her pack. The sixth morning they filled their water skins and headed to the northwest.

The first water hole was but a short day's journey, but the small pool was scummy. Carl was checking the ground around the pool while Janan was cleaning out the small spring. "Just a few small tracks, sis. How is the water?"

Janan stood watching the small stream of water clear where it came from under a large rock. "Looks clean enough." She dipped a handful of the water and sniffed for odors, then tasted what she held. "It smells all right. I'll drink a bit of it and wait to see what happens." She grinned, adding, "If it doesn't set well, I'll stick my finger down my throat."

Carl smiled and shook his head at her foolishness. "I see some oilwood over there that should make a good fire for our pot, and there looks to be enough dead limbs under those trees for a night fire."

After a supper of trail stew, Janan was feeling a lot better. With a full belly and a cup of strong tea, she sat watching Carl finger-measure their copy of the cave map. "Looks like a day and a half to the next one, sis. Though," he frowned at the piece of deer hide, "if we start walking as soon as it is light enough to see our feet, and push hard, we might make it in one day."

"It might be for the best, Carl. I don't like the idea of sleeping out on the sand. We have found no sign of big animals, but that doesn't mean there are none out here."

He nodded and went on. "The next one is southwest of there. From that one to the next is due west, and from it to the last one is a little north of west. The last two, and the river, look to be just a half day's walk apart. It looks like the river runs north and south. We can come to it from any direction unless there are hills."

She smiled and said, "We will worry about that when we get there, but the closer we get to that river, the more apt there will be animals…or men."

They found their animals at the last water hole. Squabbling over a kill were several big cats. They were tawny in color and of two kinds. Some had a bushy ruff on their neck and shoulders, while others were more slender and had none of the long hair. Janan guessed that they were male and female of the same kind.

"We can make the river before dark, sis." Carl checked the wind and motioned to the north. "Better go around that way. It's downwind, and there are some hills up that way."

Janan checked her water skin, then nodded. "Good enough. I don't want to mess with those things. We will play it by ear and see what comes.

What came was a game trail over a low range of hills and the sudden appearance of a town. The town was located in a large blind canyon on the east side of a fair-sized river. On the west bank of the river was a large camp made up of tents.

"Those huts look like the ones we build, but it is too late to go down tonight, Carl. Be dark before we could get down there. I don't think I want to walk into a strange village after dark. What we need is a good, safe lay up in a tree or something."

"Big rock over there, and it has a flat top. If we can get up there and stay flat, I doubt anyone could see us. Be kinda hard sleeping, but nothing could slip up on us."

Janan looked the way he was pointing, and blinked. Big didn't begin to describe the thing. The rock was situated on a small rise, without a tree close enough to use as a ladder. Walking that way she found the rock even more impressive. Walking around it, she could find no way to climb to the top.

"Well, Carl, what now?"

"Rope."

"Too short."

"I'll tie mine to yours, then tie a rock on one end and throw it over. You take that end and find something to take a couple of turns around while I climb. You are lighter than I am, sis, so I can anchor while you climb."

"That'll do! Let's get to it before it gets too dark to see."

Dawn was just showing when Janan came awake, sudden and quiet. Carl had laid a hand on her shoulder.

"Men," he hissed in her ear.

Janan rolled quietly out of her blankets to listen, then to slip to the side of the rock closest to the game trail they had walked the day before. In the pearly light, men were moving in a single file. They were armed men making no sound other than the quiet scuff of boots on soil. She tried to count, but they were gone.

Carl whispered, "'Bout fifty, and up to no good." He slid over to look toward the river.

Janan joined him. She could catch glimpses of the men among the trees. The camp across the river was quiet, as was the town, but she saw a man on the heights above the town. He was standing guard, holding a long spear. She was thinking hard, almost sure the town held her people, and it looked like they were about to be attacked. If the raiders took out the watchman, it would be a complete surprise.

The sound of a screech owl broke the silence of the morning, scaring Carl half to death. Janan sat upright with her hands to her mouth, then the call of a night hawk broke from her hands. Below, the watchman turned their way and raised his spear. From the hands of Carl's half sister, he heard the cry of a hunting red-tailed hawk.

"Come on, Carl, off this rock, quick. They went left, so we go right. Move it." Carl glanced back to the watchman, but he was gone.

Old Mathou stood in the middle of the men of the town, talking with the town leader. "Who signaled? All of us are here. Are you sure you heard a signal, not just normal bird calls?"

Mathou was frowning. "Do you think me an old fool?" This was just what some of the younger men were thinking. "I know what I know. It was the attack warning, and I don't care where it came from. Get your weapons, fools!"

There was a rumble of grumbling beginning, when the scream of a wounded man sent them running for their weapons.

Janan and Carl were in a small stand of trees, and from where they stood they could see the men of the town standing around the watchman. To the left the band of marauders had moved to a flat below. Hidden by a line of bush, they were crawling toward the town.

"Carl, it looks like those idiots are arguing with the watchman while the raiders are moving in on them."

"Yeah, and few of those around the man are armed." He eyed the slowly crawling men. "Think we better send the town another warning, another hawk squall maybe?"

"Nay, but I might be able to put an arrow in one of the skulkers. It is a long shot, but it might work."

"No big problem, sis. Do you see that one with the big fat butt sticking up? I'll bet you one gold piece I can hit a target that big."

"Sis" grinned and said, "You're on, and I will see what I can do."

***

Just as the men of the town returned carrying big boar spears, and with a plethora of knives sticking from boot tops and belts, a big, fat warrior burst from the bushes and began running in circles, an arrow sticking in one fat buttock. The rest of the attackers followed.

In the middle of the advancing men, Mathou noted men in the rear rank of their opponents falling, dead or wounded, with arrows sticking out of them. Someone with a bow and a grievance had come up behind the raiders. Then arrows began reaching between the advancing line of spear carriers; trained women and older girls had come up behind them to use longbows against the intruders.

When the line of townsmen hit the intruders, the women could no longer fire arrows; their men were in the way. Now it was spear and skinning knives against sword and knife, but the ranks of the raiders had been thinned and were getting the worst of it.

Mathou had just used the butt of his spear to down a foe when a falling raider tripped him up. When he rolled over, a raider stood over him with a sword aimed his way. Before he could defend himself, another sword knocked the descending blade away. A thin buckskin-clad figure stood with his back to Mathou, facing a surprised, heavy-built warrior. The warrior's blade was the heavier weapon, but the lighter blade was longer and kept deflecting it in a way that was leading the blade it opposed out of line. Suddenly it was over. The lighter blade tipped the warrior's blade aside and, in one motion, ran him through.

The buckskin clad swordsman stepped back and pulled at the same time, retrieving his sword. Bringing the sword to guard, the buckskin-clad figure turned, seeking another opponent. A swordswoman, not a man! Then another similarly clad but heavier-built sword-swinger joined the woman, and they engaged two more of the raiders.

Mathou climbed stiffly to his feet and picked up his boar spear, just in time to bring the butt of it down on the head of a foe trying to backstab one of the leather-clad sword-swingers. Looking for other foe, he found none. The remaining raiders were running for the line of brush, but very few made it; the bows of the town's women were being used with a deadly effect. Looking for the buckskin-clad pair, he found them cleaning their blades on some of the dead.

As Mathou limped toward the newcomers, he noted with surprise that there was blood flowing from a wound in his thigh. Before he could get to his goal, a woman descended on him and pushed him down to a sitting position. "Dammee, old man, sit down before you fall down." After slitting the seam of his trouser leg, she began cleaning and bandaging the wound. With the wound taken care of, someone handed him a big mug of wine, which he downed with one long swallowing.

Helped to his feet, Mathou looked for the newcomers just as a shout of warning and a rumble of hooves caused him to bellow, "To the barricades."

The second wave of the attack was too late, but horsemen were crowding through the narrow entrance of the canyon. The women, manning the barricades with bows, were interspersed with spearmen. As he walked the barricades, telling those with bows not to shoot the horses, Mathou noticed the newcomers had retrieved their bows and were filling their quivers from the bundles of spare arrows.

As the horsemen approached the barricades, big nets swung out from the steep walls of the canyon entrance and dumped small rocks on the riders. Those left in the saddle were met with a hail of arrows. As the few riders still horsed turned to flee, limping men ran with them. The spearmen that followed were more interested in retrieving horses than chasing men. Some horses had to be destroyed, but a few were led back through the line of barricades.

Ignoring the officious town leader, Mathou posted lookouts on high places and organized those caring for the wounded. Only then did the old hunter start looking for the buckskin-clad pair.

Ten

Mathou found the newcomers seated on low stools and being served cups of wine to go with bowls of the hot stew older women were serving those who had battled. Stopping before the pair, he looked them over. A woman and a young man. He couldn't place the age of the woman, but the man could not be over seventeen, maybe a bit more. Their buckskins showed heavy wear, and they were well armed. The boy had the look of a villager, with the distinctive features and dark hair, but the woman had a red-gold braid of hair that hung alongside her quiver. She put him in mind of another, but he could not recall who it was.

The woman arched elegant brows, then smiled and said, "Well, Mathou, do you think you will know us should we meet again?"

Mathou frowned. "How do you know my name, stranger?"

She grinned; a happy, mischievous glint in her gray eyes. "How could I not know your name, since you hunted with Jube."

His face went blank, trying to hide his surprise, then he remembered a young girl with red hair and gray eyes. "Janan!" Her eyes glistened as her smile grew. "But, but, but," Mathou stuttered, then, smiling ruefully, said, "Aye, Janan's age would have doubled...tripled. So it's you, girl. Did Jube make it?"

Eyes still sparkling, she said, "Aye, and is doing well. He sent us to find you, to see if we still had a village. Now what's going on here?"

"You ignorant old goat." An older woman held out a stool as she berated Mathou. "Get off that leg and get something to eat."

Janan laughed and said, "Heyla, Sallee. Are you still trying to tame this old woodsrunner?" While the woman looked at her with a puzzled frown, Janan turned to Carl. "This is the woman who mothered me after my ma died." She put her bowl on the ground and stood to wrap the older woman in her arms. Kissing her on the forehead, Janan held her at arms length and said, "Sal, you are looking well, but I thought you would have dumped this old goat by now."

Coming out of her shock, the older woman threw her arms around the younger, and burst into tears. "Jan, oh, Jan." She stood on tiptoe to plant a kiss on each of Janan's tanned cheeks, then lay her head on Janan's breast while she tried to regain control of her emotions.

The older woman finally stepped back and took a deep breath. "Girl, you almost gave me heart-stop." She shook her head just a little. "Look at you! So tall and so beautiful. You'd never know you were related to Jube. Is that old hellion still with us?"

Janan laughed and said, "A little gimpy, but still getting along." She grinned impishly as she held a hand out toward Carl. "But I am forgetting my manners. Let me introduce you to Carl...Jubeson."

Mathou had taken the marriage of Jube and Megan in a stride, but Sallee was all but indignant. "Surely Meg could have done better, but I guess you think she did well. She always seemed to think being a healer meant not having a man or family. Wonder why she changed her mind?"

When Janan had explained the circumstances, without saying where the two had hidden, Sallee shook her head dubiously and said, "Meg had as much to do with your raising as I did. After your ma, Jube would not take another woman. Meg seemed determined not to take a man, but seemed to like mothering you. I wonder why the sudden change of heart?"

Mathou surprised his wife by answering her question. "Guess it was kinda lonesome like, just the two of them." He turned to Janan with a question. "What happened to you and our village? Is that Antore still on the rampage, or has someone killed that dog's get?"

Janan held nothing back as she explained the past years. She told of Antore claiming a kingdom, and of how Jube's little group had trained to be a warrior band. "Antore keeps away from the wood south of the plain. He has sent army a couple of times, but that has cost him men. They have not found our lay-up."

"And your daughters be Antoredottir?"

The grey eyes held nothing of humor, but did hold a spark that bode nothing good for Antore. "Nay, Mathou, they be Janandottir. And Jube and Jubedottir both have arrows with Antore's name on them."

"Well," the old woodsman shrugged, "that be your business."

That evening all but those on guard or prowling the river bank sat around a central fire listening to the newcomers talk with Mathou, who was saying, "It was a good thing that you remembered the old signals, girl. I think your warning saved our butt. I think they planned to hit us from behind when their horses charged the barrier. Now then, you say that our land is at peace now? Could we rebuild our village and live as we once did, or perhaps move to that safe place Jube has found?"

"I think you could move back there and be safe enough. Antore only does battle with bandits now. That and guards his northern border. He encourages trade, and the traders, because he keeps the bandits down, give him voice support."

Janan let the last part of his question slide and asked, "So, how do you fare in this new land, and what about these raiders?"

Mathou accepted a cup of the hot tea that was being served, then narrowed his eyes and sipped. Finally he answered, "We have not fared well. There are several roving tribes on the plains to the west of the river. At our back the sand desolation seems to have no end, north or south. At our first contact with the tribes, all our horses and much of our livestock were stolen. We think of moving back to the wildwood, between the sand and our old village, but without draft horses we could take just what we could carry on our backs. We have little enough left. We can lose no more and still have enough to build a village."

Carl looked up and said with his usual brevity, "Take horses from that bunch across the river?"

Mathou turned to him with a curt nod and said, "Aye, we might. We beat them up bad today, and we have had to learn the way of a warrior band. We were always a peaceful people, needing just enough arms to fend off bandits. We know not sword work; but spear, bow and knife, we know. But there may be another way. We do not cut the throats of prisoners, as the plains tribes do among themselves. It may be that we can trade prisoners for horses." He glanced at Janan. "Do you two ride?"

"Nay." She grinned. "But you will find us willing learners."

He chuckled. "Aye, you be a Jubedottir." Mathou's face became expressionless. "We are patching up their men, and I expect to see the bitch who leads them coming under a truce by sun high tomorrow. I have never seen it, because those tribes seem to fight each other at the drop of a hat, but they might band together to fight a common foe."

Janan's brows were up. "A woman leads them!"

"Aye, and because they have a religion that venerates the Crone, they count women higher than a man."

It was quiet around the fire for some time, then Carl became downright verbose. "Jokome told of a religion that worshiped the four aspects of a goddess, and one of them was the crone." He grinned. "Heyla, sis, you couldn't be the maid, but you could be the mother. Didn't you bring a new set of buckskins with you?"

Before she could answer Carl's foolishness, Mathou spoke up. "So Jokome is still trading. Does he still try to look like an old granther?"

Carl nodded. "And Jube names him 'old thief,' yet. Sis says that was how Jube named him when she was just a lass."

Mathou was chuckling when he spoke. "That he did." Then he lost all humor. "Lad, your idea might be worth thinking on." In the surprised silence that followed, the crackling of the fire was the only sound until he said, "Aye, lad, your idea just might be worth thinking about. Jan, you don't look like our villagers. You take after your ma, who Jube found way south and brought home to the village."

While Mathou sat in thought, the men and women of the village sat talking quietly. Most of the children were asleep or near to it. Men and women talked quietly of their old home and of the newcomers; several remembered Janan, but among those still in their girlhood there was giggling and whispering.

"Carl," Janan whispered to her half brother, "you are getting a lot of attention. Have you picked out a wife yet?" Even in the firelight she could see his face redden.

She was trying to keep her chuckles quiet when Mathou again spoke. "I think it would be for the best if we leave this place. After this day the tribes may decide they need us dead or enslaved. I think it best that we return east across the sands before messengers from this tribe can bring other tribes. I don't know that they would join together for battle, but I have no wish to wait around to see if they would. With the help of our villagers, who have looked for and found us, and by trading our prisoners, I think we could get the horses we need."

As the volume of conversation grew, Mathou held up one hand. "I am guide and hunter, not leader; nor want to be. As for me, if I can get horses, me and mine will be heading east as soon as may be. Tonight you must make up your mind if you go with me, and inform your leader. Discuss it with all, even those on guard. I will be in my hut with Carl and Janan. Send your decision to me there."

He nodded to Janan and Carl. "Come along, if you will, and we will talk. Bring your stools."

Sallee poured each of them a mug of wine while they settled before the older couple's fireplace. As they sipped, Mathou began talking.

"I know of the religion that Jokome was talking about. Carl just may have had a good idea."

Carl shook his head. "I was just making jest."

"Aye, lad, but you know not the tribes. When one of their leaders comes to confer with us they always bring a totem, a pole with a square of hide on it. On the hide is the likeness of a withered old woman all dressed in black. This be the crone; they know not the one God. Now I think you said that Janan has a new set of buckskins. Are they really new?"

Janan shook her head. "Not new, but spotless and well broke in."

Mathou nodded slowly. "Now, girl, the tribes have never seen your like, and some of their warriors got away in one piece having seen you in battle. Here is my thought. This be early spring, the time of the maid, and if you could play her part we might scare the pants off that old biddy who leads this tribe. They are more than a little superstitious. If our people decide what I think they will, you will need what sleep you can get. Get you some shuteye. Sal will wake you early and help you get all gussied up. Carry all your weapons and think of what you might say to that old harridan." A sneer shaped his mouth. "If we can get our leader to go along with it, we might get Sal to play leader. I will have to think about it."

The sun was rising toward noon, and a nervous Janan was practicing her part. Dressed in her spotless yellow-brown buckskins, she carried all her weapons except her bow. Dressed in his second set of buckskins, Carl acted as escort and bow carrier. With a full quiver on her back, and with newly washed and braided hair hanging in a single braid over her shoulder and down her breast, she walked to where the prisoners were held.

Mathou had explained that the aspect of the maid was virginal and chill toward men, so Janan was trying for a cold expression as she approached the prisoners. Having been coached, the guards made a sign and backed away, a solemn expression on their faces. Janan noted slight twitches at the corners of some mouths and hoped they could keep from grinning.

She stopped and looked down at the captives. They sat on the ground, their hands tied before them. They were bloodstained and dirty, except for one. Except for that one, a young man, all were sullen of expression. The boy was just as dirty, but was without wound. His expression was one of a man who liked what he saw.

Imperious, Janan motioned to one of the village men, then at the boy. When the boy had been jerked to his feet by his bound hands, Janan tried for a cold voice. "From whence came this child, to be among the prisoners?"

She noted the boy's face reddened. Then the man holding him forgot himself enough to shrug, but his voice tone was as it should be. "Honored lady, he was found unharmed and sneaking away. He carried many water skins; perhaps he is a slave and was made to carry water for the warriors." This time the red face included a frown.

Janan turned to the prisoners. "Know you, those who attack my people," she held a cupped hand before her, "that I hold your lives in my hand." She slowly turned her hand over as if pouring water from that hand. "Should I wish it, I will pour your lives into the dust. I came from there," she pointed toward the giant rock, which showed just blue sky above it, "to defend my people. Because of my elder sister, whom you worship, I have suffered your actions. Now you have gone too far. Perhaps your tribe should follow the crone at the turning."

Janan turned to stare into the eyes of the boy. "I will not sully my mouth with the tongue of your tribe, child. Tell these what I say, and see that you fully tell them my words."

Not only did the boy's mouth fall open, but also the guard's. As his eyes widened, the startled boy stammered, "How...how...how...

Janan made her smile thin and cold. "I know what I know, child. Now speak my words before I lose my patience and empty my hand!"

Completely overawed, the boy turned to speak to the prisoners. Janan turned away. As she marched toward the huts she couldn't see the grin of her half brother.

When they had walked into Mathou's hut, she slumped, let out a sigh and turned, only to see Carl's mirthful expression. She took a swipe at him, making him dodge back, then she said, "I don't know if I can keep up that charade."

"I have watched and listened. You did better than I hoped." Mathou was chuckling. "I think you may have made a convert! But how did you know the boy could speak our language?"

Janan gave him a wry smile. "His expression gave him away. I wonder where he learned our language?"

"No matter, that old harridan has crossed the river and has dismounted; she now approaches with two others. Sallee will meet her, and four young men watch Montige. He did not like my idea, so I told him that should he interfere, the village would need a new leader. The boys promised they would pull him down and tie him if he tried to join our little show. I think he will behave, because almost all have decided to go east with us; if we can get the horses, I think all will join us. Have you decided what you will say should your turn come?"

Janan frowned and shook her head slightly. "No, not exactly. I think I will just have to play it as it comes. But I also think you had better have that boy standing by to translate." She grimaced. "I have told him that I will not sully my mouth with their foul tongue."

Eleven

Sallee, with two younger women backing her, stood watching the approach of two women and a young girl. They had stopped briefly to inspect the bodies laid out at the entrance to the canyon. Now, as they continued their approach, Sal's eyes narrowed; the child had the look of a villager.

A middle-aged woman carried a totem of the Crone. Behind her walked a strong-looking woman with the stride of a warrior. By her side, and held by a shoulder, was the girl.

Sallee spoke without turning her head. "Go tell Janan that the girl is one of ours, stolen about two years ago."

One of her escort walked the short distance to a group of village women, who stood armed and watching. Janan stood in the rear of the group, a dark shawl covering her hair, and another, her buckskins. The escort stopped a moment, then returned.

The returning woman arrived just before the totem was planted and held against the breeze coming from the river. The leader of the plains people marched the girl around the totem and faced the banner. The woman raised one hand and howled a screeching chant, then bowed low, forcing the girl to follow suit; then they faced the village.

When the plains woman had spoken, the girl translated. "Hail, old woman, from Leader Lamoa. The body count is twelve short. Do you have prisoners, or do you keep some for meat?"

Sallee looked haughtily down her nose, spoke, then waited for the translation. "Your count is wrong. We have thirteen prisoners, a number of ill fortune."

The plains leader hissed. "You lie! You will bring fourth my warriors and beg the Crone for mercy. Call on her name and swear to her your allegiance, or meet our charge."

"Nay, it is not her time; it is the spring, and do you really have the warriors to spare for another charge? The turning is long moons away. All year Dains is called on, but the maid is most strong in the spring. Yesterday, from up toward the eastern sky, a woman bright as the sun came to us and did fight with us, and we did win." Sallee threw up both arms and shouted, "Bright lady, we thank you for your help."

Behind the village women, Janan and Carl bent their knees so women could lift the dark coverings that hid their buckskins and lift the dark shawl that hid Janan's hair.

The plains women stared at the three village women, who each held both arms high as Sallee chanted her thanks. Seemingly in a blink, someone stood behind them, a woman. It was a woman with a long, red-gold braid falling down to divide her breasts. A woman with clothing glowing a color deeper than the color of the sun. She wore two knives and a sword. Over her shoulder could be seen feathered ends of arrows, and a quiver strap under her braid separated her breasts. As she strode past those who called, an escort followed. A dark male, yet dressed as she was, bore her bow while his bow hung from one shoulder.

The golden woman stepped to the side of Sallee, raised her arm and snapped her fingers. Her escort turned and made a motion with his hand. Women led the captive boy to the side of the golden woman and cut his bindings. Her cold glance swept over him, and he shivered. "Go to your leader, boy." Her voice was just a breath.

"But I want to stay and serve you." His voice was no louder.

The cold eyes seemed to soften for a moment, then, "Do as I say, child. Perhaps another day." The cold eyes hardened as the boy walked slowly to join his leader.

Janan tried to hold the expression on her face and in her eyes to a mild interest. The plains leader dodged out of her way as she strode up to the totem to look on the face of the crone. "Hail, sister. Your time is not yet, but I greet you with honor. You will withdraw while I deal with the problem of your followers. A virgin maid has been stolen for evil intent, and my followers have been attacked one time too often."

Janan could hear the boy stuttering as he translated, and heard the totem bearer whisper, "Dains!"

Janan backed three steps, held up one arm and said, "Farewell until the turning, elder sister."

The totem bearer stared upward, then she screamed as her overwrought imagination furnished a form. "I saw her! I saw her leave!" She fell on her face.

Janan didn't know who was more startled, herself, or the people around her. Somehow she kept her face still and cold. Not wasting the opening, she turned to the girl and said, "Come to me, girl."

When the tribal leader clutched the girl's shoulder, Janan's arm snapped straight out as she pointed a finger directly at the face of the woman. Startled, fear came to her face, and her grip loosened. The girl wrenched free and ran to Sallee, who wrapped her in a hug and whispered urgently in her ear.

The plains leader stared at Janan; hate was warring with fear until the hate overcame the fear. She drew the sword she was wearing.

Janan had been expecting something like this. Zackoro's instructions rang in her mind as she lightly met the woman's sword, then rolled into a bind. The opposing sword flew to one side, and Janan's blade was pointed at her opponent's heart. Her cold voice came softly. "You know what you deserve, woman."

When the boy was silent, the girl followed the instructions whispered by Sallee. She knelt in the dust to one side, where she could see Janan's face. With a look of awe on her face, she translated.

The older woman was stunned by a sword play she had never encountered before. Slowly she slipped to her knees and bowed her head. "I was wrong, oh Dains. Forgive my ignorance."

Janan stepped back, sheathed her sword, looked at the boy and said, "Take up the blade of your leader and bear it for her until you are out of my sight." With the girl translating, she said to the plains woman, "Rise, take your dead to your camp; return with two good horses for each captive held by my people. Try not my forbearance. When I have led my people from this accursed ground you may light the funeral pyres and call for the return of she whom I banished. Her time is at the turning, but I have my strength until then."

In Mathou's hut the young girl huddled on a stool before the fireplace, awe still written on her face, even as Janan sat on another stool with a bad case of the shakes.

"How in the name of all that is holy did we do that?"

Sallee, pouring wine for all, even a small cup for the girl, shook her head. "All I can think of is that your words and actions must have come from the one God." She turned to hand the small cup of wine to the rescued girl. "Here, Nan, drink this, but not too fast. Your ma should be here any minute, so don't drink it too slow either."

Nan saw her mother coming through the doorway, and gulped the wine. The unaccustomed drink choked her, and tears ran down her face as her mother swept her off the stool to smother her with hugs and kisses. "Leggo, Mamma, yer smothering me."

Sallee rescued the girl and used a wet cloth to wipe both the wine and tears from her face. But her mother clung to one hand, almost incoherent. "Nannie, oh Nannie, did they hurt you? Are you all right?"

"I'm all right, Ma. I'm all right. They just made me work hard and learn to talk their words. They made me teach our words to that boy, too. Got thumped a few times, though, for not doing to suit them, but I'm all right." She turned big eyes on Janan. "This goddess saved me. I've never seen a goddess before, Ma."

Janan was halfway into her cup of wine, and had settled down some. She smiled at the young girl. "And I am afraid you have not seen one this day, Nan. I am just a woman who was playing like I was something I am not. We just wanted to scare those other people, and we scared them a lot more than we thought we could." She looked at Sallee. "I hope Mathou is getting things organized. We need to get out of here before that old heifer has too much time to think about what happened."

Mathou, Janan, Carl and two young men armed with bows stood above the canyon, watching the camp across the river. The villagers had worked all night to move out at dawn. With women archers and spearmen on guard, they had moved south, down the river, to turn east just below the camp on the west side of the river.

When the last cart and the last of the rear guard had passed into the trees, big fires grew to the west of the tent encampment. After the prisoner exchange the previous afternoon, the watch told of three riders leaving that encampment. What the villagers could not know were the tales told about Janan that night by the prisoners and the boy; nor was the overwrought totem bearer silent.

"Mathou, I think we should push hard and bypass that first water hole. It will be hard on the stock, but they can rest a night at the second water hole." Janan then turned to Carl. "And I think we will go back to where we slept the other night and put on one last show."

When she turned back to the older man, Mathou had tilted his head to one side and had one brow raised in question. Janan ginned at him. "That big rock on the hill above the canyon was our bed that night. It was from that rock we first caught sight of the skulkers, and it was from there we signaled you. I think I will flash my sword a few times from the top of that rock, then drop out of sight."

For long moments Mathou studied her through narrowed eyes, then nodded. "Aye, and I will take my guards and my gimpy leg down to that blasted pony cart." He glared at the young men, who grinned. "Don't tarry, Jan. I want you with the train before we get to that first water hole. I have an idea I want to try. One that should slow any who might follow us."

When they arrived at the gigantic rock, Janan, using the doubled ropes again, climbed to the top of it. Standing on the western side of the boulder, she drew her sword and let the sun flash off the bright blade. She held her pose until there were several people watching her from the west side of the river. Sheathing her blade, she backed to the east side of the boulder and threw her hands high. Holding that pose for long moments, she dropped her arms, grabbed the rope and slid down the eastern face of the rock.

Carl quickly joined her with the ropes already separated. Without a word they coiled their lariats and, hanging them on their belts, made their way to the game trail. They then headed east at the ground covering lope Jube had taught all in his family.

When they caught up with the tail of the caravan, Mathou waved them over to his pony cart. "Did ye get their attention, girl?"

Janan grinned. "Aye, but I have no idea if it will give them pause. Did you warn the guards about those big cats?"

Mathou nodded. "Yes, and since the wind is out of the northeast, I told them to stay well south of the water hole. I don't think the cats will attack us. When we came through heading west our scouts warned us, and even though we stopped to water our stock, they stayed away. Too many of us, at a guess."

"So what is your idea for slowing down any would-be followers." Janan raised her elegant brows. "If they get help from other tribes they may come looking for trouble."

Mathou gave Janan a thin grin. "I had young Jocko, Mebee and Thom's oldest boy draw your picture on a big square of hide. Jocko does pretty well with pigments. We will make that into a totem similar to what the tribes use, and we'll plant that in the middle of our track just before we get downwind of the water hole." Chuckling, he added, "As we pass that water hole we'll put a big ox down and leave it for the cats. Girl, did ye ever see big cats guarding a kill?" His laugh was cold. "I wouldn't want to be among their scouts."

At the second water hole Montige was still trying to play the role of leader. "Man and beast need at least a two-day rest. In this sand we cannot keep up this pace."

The caravan had stopped at the water hole, and small fires burned along the strung-out wagons and carts. Mathou stood looking down at the small, tubby village leader. "When all are fed and watered and have had three hours rest, we go on. We have the blessing of a full moon to travel by. The brush we have been dragging will do much to confuse the trail. I doubt they will be able to trail us by night. Also, I doubt they know where the water holes are located, so they may completely lose our track if they try to trail at night. If they do try to follow at night, their horses will muddy where our track turns more northerly."

"But this pace will kill the animals," Montige blustered. "I forbid it!"

"Better dead animals than dead people, but ye may do as you wish." Mathou gave him a wry smile. "As for me and any that wish to go with me, we will march in three hours." His smile turned grim. "Any who wish may stay and greet the plains warriors."

By noon the next day both animal and man were faltering. Janan was walking with Carl alongside Mathou's pony cart. Looking up, she said, "We must rest tonight, old man."

He looked back down the caravan's line and nodded. "Aye." He again nodded his head. "A full night of rest. After that we turn northeast and, if we do a good job of covering our trail, we should lose them if anyone still follows." Mathou shrugged his wide shoulders. "If anyone *has* been following. I sent Dondro to the north of our track; far enough to lose himself in the distance, but close enough to spot a large band following. If he must, he will kill his horse getting us word of any band that follows us."

Food, water and a long night's sleep worked wonders for both man and beast. Dondro had come in near midnight with a good report. No one was yet on their trail. While all were eating a breakfast of trail stew, Mathou and a group of lead warriors were discussing the situation; Janan and Carl listened.

"Well, old woodsrunner," a tall, muscular man was saying, "it looks like no one is trailing us. Your plan seems to have worked."

Mathou sat frowning over his bowl of stew. Shaking his head slightly he said, "We be not out of the wood, yet." Then he lifted his chin and gave a small, grim smile. "Or sand, if ye will. This will be the long leg of our journey, and we will have to sleep on the way tonight. Pass the word that it will be a cold camp with no fires. Dondro will finish his sleep in his wagon, then take up his station to the north of us. If no one is following, we will go on to the last water hole tomorrow."

Happy was the day when the hills of the eastern Desolation rose before them. A ragged cheer went up, but that was all the tired villagers could muster.

The caravan made camp at the first good creek in the wildwood. With good forage and water for the animals, the villagers were happy to begin setting up a semi-permanent camp. Skilled hunters were gone but two hours before bringing back meat. Going out with some of the older women, who remembered what to look for, youngsters found and brought back fruit, greens and tubers.

While the village folk settled in, Mathou organized those who would keep an eye on the sand to the west. From the heights of the last spur of hills, two men would be on watch day and night.

Twelve

Trade had been good, but had slowed to nothing by mid-afternoon. Jokome decided he had earned a rest, a bath and a good meal. He started closing up his wagon and locking it tight; nearby traders would keep an eye on it. Coming from the far side of the wagon, he glanced up the line of wagons and stalls just in time to see a slight pair of figures turning into an alley that held just trade stalls. Both wore buckskins, and each had a blond braid hanging down her back.

Dee was behind a rack of clothing, putting her purchases in the light pack she had brought, when a group of four armed soldiers marched by the cloth dealer's stall. She and Lee had divided the coins Lee had brought, then Lee had gone on up the way, seeking the dealer in blades the cloth merchant had mentioned. Dee thought she had bargained well, getting two gowns for two silvers, not knowing the merchant would have settled for one.

She had settled the pack and stepped into the way to watch the receding backs of the soldiers, when a heavy hand descended on her shoulder. Wrenching away and turning, her sword was halfway out of its sheath when she saw who had grabbed her shoulder.

"Jokome!" She eased the blade back into the sheath.

He shoved her back in among the hanging clothing. "Which are you, and where is the other one?"

"Lee went up the way to find a blade merchant. Why?" She had never seen such a scowl on the trader's face.

"What are you two hellions doing here? Who came with you? Don't you know you are in danger here? How did you come to be here?" His expression caused Dee to step back a pace.

"Just us two, and we just came to do some trading. W-why?" She stuttered a little. "W-what danger?"

Jokome squinted his eyes. "Does Jube know you are here?"

"N-no, we didn't decide to come up here until we got to the trace." Dee's voice rose. "What are you so excited about, anyhow?"

He didn't answer, but turned to the cloth merchant. "Eain, traders' emergency. Do you have two light cloaks with hoods, about the size of this one?"

"Aye, Jokome. Two cloaks that are lightweight, black and cheap." He glanced at Dee. "Is this the one he be looking for?"

"No, but his men will not know that."

Eain nodded sagely. "Aye, she be about what he favors."

Lee was bargaining for a strong, long, thin, two-edged fighting knife when two hands gripped her shoulders. Surprising her captor with her strength, she jerked away and turned on him, the long blade at ready.

The soldier she had turned on jumped back. "Be careful with that thing, girl." He scowled at the chuckling of the soldiers beside him, then turned back to the armed girl. "Don't you know better than to draw a blade on the king's guard?"

"Don't you know better than to grab a woman from behind, especially when she is dickering for a blade?" Lee frowned, then added, "What you want?" She moved her wrist a little, making the blade wag from side to side. "Speak up before I decide to give you a second smile for attacking me."

"Now, now, girl," the oily voice of the weapon merchant came from behind her, "these did not attack you. Ye did react too strongly. Now mind your manners and answer the guard's questions."

She glanced behind her quickly, then back to the guards. The merchant did not have a knife in his hand, but a half-sword was right by that hand. Seeming to relax, she smiled brightly at the four guards. "Aye, I'll be right with you." Lee turned to the merchant with a thin grin on her face, and flipped the knife in the air. It came down, point first, between his hand and the half sword.

She turned back to the guards to once more give them a bright smile. "Now, what can I do for you big, strong soldiers?"

The knife merchant had snatched his hand away from the quivering blade, and the guard who had been doing all the talking was chuckling at his discomfort.

Still grinning, the leader of the guards said, "Well, young lady, if you will step over here we can talk without long ears listening in."

When the four tried to close around her, Lee put her back against the wall of a stall. "Na, na, none of that." One of the guards was not much older than Lee, so she chose him. "Why don't you three go on ahead; this'n can walk with me. He's plumb pretty."

While the younger guard turned red, the others laughed uproariously and the leader said, "Aye, Lenderson, you escort this dangerous suspect. Watch her close and don't let her get away."

A few paces up the lane the soldiers halted. "Now, young woman, you will answer a few questions. The guard has orders to be on the lookout for certain people, and you might be one of them. First, where do you come from and what are you here for?"

Now Lee was impulsive, but she was not slow. Adding a bit to the brogue she affected, she said, "Well, now, ah come in from the wood for a bit o' tradin'."

"What wood? Where do you live?"

"In the wood west o' here, right back agin the Desolation. Why would you be lookin' for me?"

"Never mind that. What is your name?"

" 'Tis Lee."

"Is that all there is to it?"

She gave him a sour look. "Every girl ain't lucky enough to have a da to give her his name. You're pretty bad nosey, ain't you?"

The senior guard frowned. "Maybe." He regarded her soberly, then said, "I think you had better come along with us."

"Where to?"

"I think the king will want to talk with you."

Trying to appear as impulsive as she usually was, Lee brightened. "Hey, I never seen a king before. What would he want to be a-talkin' to me for?"

His smile was a bit sour, when the senior guard shook his head and said, "I'm not all that sure he does."

When they tried to box her in again, she reacted the same way. "Na, na, I told you none o' that." She smiled up at the younger guard. "He can escort me."

The other three grinned at the young warrior's red face, and the senior guard said, "All right, Ivor, 'escort' the young lady."

As they walked, Lee tried to keep a bright-eyed, pleased expression on her face as she looked for an escape route. But the other three warriors walked abreast, right behind her.

When Jokome and Dee arrived in the lane near the knife shop, Jokome saw who was running the place and took in his expression. Looking across the way, he guided Dee to a cook shop, where he purchased two cups of tea.

"Keep your hood up, girl, and listen to the gossip. I wouldn't trust that son of a mule at the knife shop as far as I could throw him. If anything has happened we will hear about it. If not, we will keep looking. If we hear nothing, I can ask on up the way."

What Jokome heard sent them on their way, and soon they turned west on a wide way that led to the castle of King Antore. They hurried, not knowing what they would do if they caught up with Lee and her escort, but they arrived at the square before the castle entrance just in time to see her pass through the guarded entrance of the edifice.

Dee started with determination after her sister until Jokome grabbed her arm and jerked her away. "What do you think you are doing, you little fool!"

She tried to pull away, but Jokome was stronger than he looked. He wrapped an arm around her shoulders to force her to walk to the south side of the square, where he firmly pushed her to a seat on a stone bench.

"Dee, there is no way we can get in that door, nor can we help Lee by getting ourselves caught by Antore's guards."

"But we gotta do something. Why did they take her in that place, anyhow?"

Jokome sat next to her and took her hand. "Dee, now you know why I was so angry when you showed up here. Didn't your mother tell you that Antore had his men primed to bring in any woman wearing buckskins and weapons? I warned her he was on the lookout for her and that his men were told to watch for a woman dressed like you."

"We gotta get her out of there. We gotta start home by sundown!"

He wrapped an arm around her shoulders and hugged her tight. "If she is quick-witted, she may walk right back out. She is much too young to be the one Antore is looking for, but…"

"But what!"

Jokome sat looking at her upturned face for a time before saying. "I'm sorry, Dee, but he may keep her as he kept Janan."

"But he can't do that! They hang a man for bedding his daughter. Megan said so."

He shook his head. "Antore doesn't know she is his daughter, and I am not sure he would care. If he knew, he would try to make her tell where Janan is." Jokome shook his head. "What a mess!"

"Well, we have to do something!" Dee was looking at the main entrance to the castle again.

"Tell you what, Dee, we will go over to the walk."

"What's that?"

"The walk is where people go to walk, or sit, hoping to catch a glimpse of the king. The balcony of his throne room is there, and he sometimes speaks to the people from that balcony. Come along." Jokome had no hope, but had to do something to keep Dee from doing something crazy.

Lee was actually enjoying her tour of the palace as they walked down a long, wide and a high-ceilinged hall. In four different places there were wide doorways with a thing like a metal gate hanging from the ceiling. "What's that?" she said, pointing.

Her young guard said "It is called a portcullis."

"What's it for?"

"It keeps people out that we don't want in. Now be still!"

Lee had never heard of, let alone seen, a throne room. She wondered at the oversized chair. Her escort marched her to the center of the room, then took up positions against a wall that faced the throne. After waiting for what seemed to be a long time, she started wandering around, looking at things. The big throne was well cushioned and ornate. There were rich hangings on the walls interspersed with elaborate shields. Candles burned everywhere on the walls, and on a big hanging thing in the center of the room. There was plenty of light.

Finally she walked out on a balcony. From that height she could see far down the plain. Below was a wide walk between the castle wall and the top of the outer wall of the city. A narrow stone wall sat on that outer wall, making a railing to keep people from falling off the main wall. Along the guard rail, stone benches were evenly spaced. On one bench sat a big man wearing black. Beside him a smaller figure wearing a hooded cloak was pointing at Lee. The squashed, black and dirty hat that was shoved down on the man's head was all-too-familiar.

"Get back in here!" The senior guard was scowling at her. "The king may be here at any time, and he won't want you on his balcony."

But the king was already there, standing behind a hanging with his chamberlain, who was saying, "She is much too young, sire. I don't know why she wasn't disarmed, or for that matter, why she was even brought in."

Antore chuckled, watching the swaggering young figure. "No, she is not Janan, but she might be entertaining; she is definitely not overawed. I will give her an audience. Go place her in the center of the room, then I will enter."

Lee's head came around at a slight noise. To one side of the throne an old gray head had parted the hangings to step into the room. He wore an ornate robe of green stitched with dark green embroidery. He seemed to move without walking since his robe flowed with his movement.

The old voice was melodious when he said, "Come stand here, my dear. King Antore has consented to give you an audience." Without looking, he made a summoning motion. The senior guard came to stand by the side of Lee. When the guard had stationed himself, the old man walked to the left to take a stand at one side of the throne.

To the left side of the throne, the hangings were parted for the king's entrance. As he strode to the throne, two well-dressed older warriors followed to take up a stance to the left of the throne. Antore did not sit, but stood studying the slight figure standing in the shadow of the guard captain.

Lee was startled when all but she and the old grey head gave a medium bow. Then one of the well-dressed warriors said, "Captain, why was not the prisoner disarmed?"

Before the captain could answer, the king raised his hand. "Now, now, high captain, the young lady is not a prisoner. She is too young to be the one we look for, and my subjects are allowed to come before me wearing arms. Nor am I without guards to defend me." After he had chuckled, he looked at Lee and continued. "Where is your home, and who came with you to the city?"

Lee's young nose came up. "Why?"

The chamberlain's soft voice came. "When addressing the king you should say, 'Your Majesty.' Now, answer the questions."

Antore stepped back and sat on the throne, his eyes sparkling with mirth. Lee studied him a moment before speaking. "Ah, come to get in some tradin', an' maybe look around for a man." She turned to give the younger guard a hard look. He turned red while his fellow guardsmen tried to stifle their laughter. "An' why would anybody come with me, uh...Majesty? As for me home, it be in the wood."

Only the spark in his eye showed that Antore was enjoying her brashness. "And what wood would that be, child?"

The slim figure before the throne stiffened at the word child, and a frown came with the lifting of the slightly upturned nose. "West o' here." She neglected the honorific. "Back agin the Desolation."

Antore turned to his two high captains. "I was not aware that anyone lived in that wood."

The near warrior nodded a slight bow. "There may be a few hunter families there who bring game to the market, Majesty."

Antore turned back to study Lee for some moments before saying, "Perhaps you would enjoy a stay in the palace, girl. I think you would enjoy the stay."

Lee suddenly turned and paced three steps toward the balcony. Head down, as though in thought, she turned and paced back to her guard. Repeating the action, she stopped at the far end of her march and looked at the king. "I have heard talk of you, Majesty." The brogue was quite gone, and she was looking him in the eye. "Maybe you have in mind to take me for a bed mate?" While everyone in the room, except those speaking, frowned. Lee stood, brows raised, looking at the king.

The spark was gone from Antore's eye. His face was expressionless as he said, "And would that suit you, to have that honor?"

Matching his expression, she asked a question in a deadpan voice. "Tell me, do they still hang a man for bedding his own daughter?"

His eyes narrowed. "Yes, that is the law."

"Then I think we better forget the bedding." She turned and walked toward the young guard, loosening the rope at her belt. "But why don't I rope this one and take him home with me? You seem to have a lot of extras."

"Come back here!" As she turned to face the king, Lee saw no mirth in his eyes. "Do you claim to be Antoredottir?"

She slowly shook her head. "Nay…I be Leeta…Janandottir."

Antore's expression held no warmth. "Where is your mother, girl?"

"Oh, back in the wood. She moved us up here quite a while back. Said she had a gift for you that she wanted to deliver in person."

Lee again started prowling, swinging the loop of her rope and glancing at the young guard, who was too shocked to blush. Stopping to look back at the blank expression of the king, she pulled a coin from her belt pouch. "Ma said to give you this," she said, flipping the coin in a great, high arc toward the throne.

Every eye followed the turning coin as it reflected the light from the candles. It landed right in front of the throne, bounced and came to rest with the diagonal slashed name up.

Antore stared at the coin, then roared, "Seize her!" But there was no one to seize.

The guards looked wildly around the room, but one of the high captains was calm and spoke in a normal voice tone. "Two of you search this room. Captain, take one man and check the passage to the main gate." He turned to the chamberlain. "Could she have gone into the private quarters?"

The old man shook his head. "No, the latch must move in a certain manner before the door will open."

The two guards searching the throne room were looking behind the hangings and into various nooks, even in the large urns, when the youngest guard glanced at the balcony and froze. Shaking off his amazement, he ran to look over the balcony rail, where he saw a rope trailing down the wall almost to the walk below. An old man in black stood looking over the side of the outer wall.

"You, old man," the guard shouted. When the old man turned to look around, the guard shouted, "Up here!" When the man below looked up, he continued. "Did you see a girl wearing leather?" When the old man nodded his head, the guard called down to him, "Where did she go?" When the old man pointed over the wall, the guard told him to sit on the bench behind him and not to move until a guardsman told him to move.

Antore walked out on the balcony to look at the dangling rope. Shaking his head in honest admiration he said, "A slippery little vixen."

Thirteen

Dee grabbed Jokome's arm. "That was Lee up there. Let's go!"

The trader measured the distance to the balcony with his eye. "Go where?"

"You're no help at all," Dee said. Standing, she took the lariat from her belt. "We'll go up and get her. See where that square post sticks up above the rail. I can rope it, climb up and yell at her to run, then we both slide down and run for it."

"Sit down, Dee!"

"But…"

"Girl, I doubt your rope is that long, nor is there any way you could throw your loop that far, but I think she saw us down here. I think she knows we are here." He glanced back at the main square, where he could just see where the stair from the main entrance came to the floor of the square. "If she comes back to the square we will see her. If she signals us from the balcony, we will be able to see that also. I don't think she is a prisoner, for she was still armed. Patience, Dee, patience."

Finally Jokome stood. "Time to go, Dee. We can wait no longer. I can at least get one of you out of this city."

She jumped to her feet, and faced him. "No! One way or another I am going after Lee. If you wan…"

Jokome's head jerked toward the balcony. When Dee spun around she saw a small figure coming down the wall of the castle.

The trader's quick mind jumped to a solution to an unuttered problem. "Loop the end of this bench and go over the wall, quick. Lee will be right behind you." As with her sister, Dee was not slow. As she went over the wall, she saw Lee drop the last three body lengths of her descent. Her rope was that much too short.

Jokome saw the girl hit the stone walk. With slightly bent knees taking the shock, she rolled and came to her feet, running.

"Quick, Lee, over here and over the wall. Dee is waiting below." She didn't even answer as she swarmed over the wall.

Again the rope was short, and Lee dropped the last two lengths. She hit damp earth, and again rolled. She came to her feet and the arms of Dee. After a quick hug, they both looked up, waiting for Jokome. What came down the wall was a bundle of dark cloth, followed by the trader's voice.

"Put that on, then both of you run toward the trace gate. Partway there is a stinking marsh that drains rain water and sewage from the city. There are reeds that will hide you, but don't go into the marsh. There is a length-wide stone ledge between the wall and the marsh. Stay on that until you are well hidden, then hunker down. When it is dark, come out the way you went in, then head south. Stay off the trace, move slow, keep your heads down and your blades out. I will meet you at the plains campsite. Now go!"

When the guardsman had finished shouting at him, Jokome leaned back over the railing to look for the girls, but they had gone. Jokome shook his head just a little. They were a bit argumentative and hard headed, normally, but seemed to know when to turn off the foolishness.

Zackoro had not waited too long, but set off two days after he had missed the twins. When he arrived where the cave opening overlooked the end of the wood and the beginning of the plain, he climbed to the hidden slit to hide his candle lamp. In the high slit in the wall of the cave he found not only spare candles and the twins' lamps, but two bows and quivers.

Producing a steady stream of quiet curses, some colorful and some improbable, he studied the wood below, then the plain. In the distance was a small cloud of dust raised by a troop of riders. Nearing the wood was a trader's wagon.

Two of the guards confronted Jokome. The younger guard asked the questions. "You said that you saw the girl! Where did she go?"

Jokome stared at him a long moment, his mouth hanging open. "Uh, it went over the wall like some big spider."

The guards followed him to the wall and looked where Jokome pointed. "It hit the ground and bounced, then it runned like a wild hare."

"Which way?" The younger guard was hanging over the wall, looking at the trailing rope.

Jokome pointed west. "Last I saw it runned that way, fast, like a wild doe, it did."

"Horses!" the second guard yelled. They both ran toward the square, Jokome trailing along behind them.

With all the noise and shouting, a small crowd gathered to watch a five-troop ride toward the trace gate. The trader mingled with the crowd, and left with them when the guard captain ordered the square cleared.

Fortunately the bath house that Jokome was want to frequent was without other customers when he walked in. "Heyla, Jokome. Been a while! What can I do for you?"

"Too long, Gunter. I am in a bad need of a trim and bath."

"Aye, I can see that. Come over here and shed your coat, hat and shirt. If you would let me give you a good trim you would no' have to be trimmed so often."

"That is what you always say." Jokome grinned at the barber, then he raised his brows. "I think I will take your advice this time. I've been about to smother in this heat."

The barber brightened. "Most wear both beard and hair short now, especially in the summer. If you'd let me do it that way, you'd clean up proper, I be thinkin'"

Jokome managed a chuckle. "As you will, Gunter. If I don't like it, it will grow back by the time I return."

"Leaving us already?"

"Aye, been good trading. If I get the jump on the others I'll get good prices down south, and buy at a better price."

The twins had found the ledge, but the smell was almost overwhelming. At Dee's suggestion they wet rags with water from their small water skins, and tied them over mouth and nose.

They were far enough along the ledge to be well hidden, when Lee, who was in the lead, stopped. "Someone else is out here!"

"Shh, not so loud!" They both stared at the figure seemingly asleep on a pile of straw.

Dee pulled on her sister's arm, and whispered, "Let's move back a ways and hunker down. We won't be here very long."

Lee's answering whisper came with a nod. "Aye, but we will hold bare swords under these capes, and watch both ways."

Daylight was beginning to dim when a second figure approached the one asleep, stopping well out of reach of the sleeper. The girls heard a murmur, and the sleeper came awake with a knife in one hand. The two men settled on the straw and made a meal out of the sack the second man had brought.

Dee was getting nervous as the light dimmed further. Every once in a while she could see the lighter color of a face being turned their way. "Hist, Lee, let's get out of here." Lee was suddenly of the same opinion, when she saw the two figures creeping their way.

The two men on the ledge had unsavory ways of earning their bread. When the second had brought back food for the two of them, he noted two dark-clad figures seated on past his mate's sleeping pallet. When they finished eating, the two held a whispered consultation. When they rose, to creep toward the dark figures, each held a long, sharp knife. As the skulkers approached, both dark figures rose. A long, bright blade appeared from one of the dark cloaks, then one from the other cloak. A hoarse and muffled voice sounded from the direction of those holding sword blades at ready.

"Aye, see, sister, more garbage to feed our pool." The two blades flickered in the last light of the day.

The thieves froze, then one of them yelled, "Marsh walkers!"

As Lee later told it, "They stood not on the order of their going."

Moving quickly, but silently, the twins made their way back to solid ground and across an open space to a small stand of trees. Well back in the trees, they stopped and tried to muffle their giggles.

"Wonder what a marsh walker is," said Lee with a giggle.

Catching her breath, Dee said, "I don't know, but whatever it is those two didn't want to be around a couple of them."

Lee opened her mouth to reply, but grabbed Dee's arm instead. "Shh." She had heard the sound of horses. The horses were on the open space between the city wall and the trees. Moving toward the city gate, the riders seemed to be grumbling. When the sound of the riders faded, the pair turned south with one accord, moving in the silent lope their grandfather had taught them. At moondown they stopped in a cluster of small boulders.

When Jokome approached the city gate the two guards were more interested in their conversation about the happenings of the night before than an old trader. Wearing his black clothing with the dirty old hat pulled low, he flashed the required slip, when one of the disinterested guards asked for Jokome's tax receipt. After passing through the gate, he kept to a slow, steady pace. When well out of sight of the city, he encouraged his team to a faster pace.

The twins had to lie flat to stay hidden. The rocks here were not very big. The trader had arrived when the sun was high, and that same sun was bearing down on the hidden girls. The trader was not Jokome.

While the trader staked his team out to graze, the thirsty pair gazed longingly at the stream just south of the camp. When the trader set up his pot, the smell of stew had their stomachs growling.

"Let's go see if we can buy some of that stew. We are two to his one," Lee whispered. Dee held her down.

"What's he doing?"

They watched the trader climb to the seat of the wagon, then on to the top of the vehicle. Facing north, and shading his eyes with one hand, he looked back up the trace, then he turned to the West and looked down on the hidden pair. "All right, come on in and get some food. We will be on our way as soon as the horses have rested." Stunned, they rose from their concealment and walked slowly toward the camp, swords in hand.

The trader's back was to them when they arrived, but not for long. Leaving off stirring the contents of the pot, he turned to face them. Looking at the dirty, bedraggled pair, he laughed. "You are a sorry-looking twosome." He turned back to the pot, saying, "As soon as we get some food in us, I will hitch up the team while you two clean up the pot and bowls. I won't run my team to death, but I want you two in the wood as soon as may be."

While they ate, Lee and Dee stared at the stranger. He wore relatively new clothing, brown boots, dark brown trousers and shirt, and a light brown vest covered with dark brown embroidery. Finally, Lee could no longer stand the glint of humor that showed in his eyes.

"All right. Who are you and how did you know we were here?"

Then Dee added her bit. "I don't see any reason to put up with him laughin' at us. Why don't we just rope and tie him?"

The trader said nothing, just walked to the side of the wagon and opened a hidden door. Taking out an old black hat, he jammed it on his head and scowled at them. "You can't rope me, because you two hellions left your ropes at the palace." Putting the old hat away, he resealed the hidden door and turned back to them. "Now don't give me any more of your lip. I have had about all the trouble out of you two I can stand."

The twins sat with open mouths while Jokome went for the horses. After Lee's mouth snapped shut, she opened it again to whisper, "It *is* Jokome, isn't it?"

Dee's eyes were big. "He did clean up pretty," she breathed.

As the wagon neared the wood, Lee was taking her turn at watching behind them. The twins had been taking turnabout watching the trace behind the wagon. All afternoon they had interspersed their watching with questions; when they were not ragging Jokome about how "pretty" he had cleaned up, of course.

96

The trader found himself enjoying their banter, even as he pretended a disgruntlement. "Mind your mouth, girl. I didn't clean up for your amusement. If the guard catches up with us they will be looking for an older man with long beard and hair, wearing black. Down south this is what I usually wear."

"As may be." Dee grinned at him. "I can't wait to see what happens when Ma sees you. She may just decide to add you to our family."

"Dust, way back."

"How far, Lee?"

"I can't see what's making the dust."

"All right. I will stop in the edge of the wood, then you two make yourselves scarce. If it is another trader, I will join up with him."

Dee looked up at him. "And if the dust is made by Antore's men?"

His smile was grim. "Then I will be a trader who came on the trace from that road that comes in from the east. I've seen no old traders dressed in black, nor have I laid eyes on a wildwood girl."

Fourteen

Carl was seated under the cooling branches of a large tree with a crowd of villagers near his own age, very much enjoying himself, when he saw Janan and Mathou trotting out of camp. Not wanting to leave the admiring glances of a certain young lady, he hesitated but finally said, "I'll be back," and jumped to his feet to run after his half sister.

A little winded from his run to catch up, Carl said, "What's the hurry, sis?"

It was Mathou who answered, "Signal from the lookouts."

They arrived at the base of the lookout hill just as one of the men on duty came off the path from the overlook and strolled to meet them.

"What's the problem, Erb?"

"One man coming this way."

"Scout?"

"Don't think so. He's coming out of the west, not northwest, walking. Well, stumbling, anyway. Marc is watching to see if there are any more."

The four of them walked out to the knee of the last hill and stopped to wait, just in time to see the oncoming figure sprawl flat on his face.

Erb snorted. "Buzzard bait."

They stood silent for a moment, then Carl turned to the lookout. "Let me borrow your water skin?" When Erb shrugged and acceded to the request, Carl started walking toward the sprawled body. The others hesitated, then followed.

Carl had already rolled the man onto his back when the others arrived. Mathou grunted and said, "Tribesman, he must have got lost from the others."

Janan knelt and brushed the sand from his face, then frowned. "It's the boy! Here, help me sit him up so we can give him some water." With Carl's help she got a swallow of water down him, but he choked on it and started coughing. Janan took a bandage from her belt pouch and wet it. After she had wiped his face clean of sand, she wet the cloth again and pressed it to the boy's cracked lips.

When his eyes came open, the boy was looking right into Janan's face. His eyes widened, then he croaked, "Dains." He tried weakly to get up.

"Never mind that, lad," she said, forcing him to stay seated. Taking a small cup from her pouch, she filled it and held it to his lips. "Stay you still, and drink this." She filled the cup twice more before she said, "That is enough for now. When we are sure that will stay in your belly, we will give you some more. Now you lie back and rest."

As he lay back in the sand, Janan put the wet cloth back on his lips, then turned to Carl. "Go get some help, and rig up a stretcher."

As Carl trotted away, Mathou said, "What we be doin' with him?"

Janan glanced at Mathou, then switched her gaze to Erb. "Well, I don't think we should leave him for the buzzards."

Erb gave her a sardonic look, then snorted a dry chuckle. "Well, yourself, and I better head on back to my post and tell my watch mate about our new guest." He left Janan chuckling at his dry wit.

Sallee took the task of looking after their "guest" seriously, so it was that the next day Janan found him sitting cross-legged on his pallet. His lips were coated with a salve, and his clothing was clean and mended.

Ducking into the tent, she stopped to look him over. "No, stay put," she said, stopping his effort to rise. After a further study of his face, she started questioning him, a neutral expression on her face and in her voice, "Well, boy, do you want to tell me how you came to be here? Start with your crossing the river."

"Gregor." The voice came from near the tent's entrance. Sallee was seated on a stool there.

"What?"

"He is named Gregor, and he is not a boy. About Carl's age, I would say. A bit scrawny for his age, but he should feed up right well."

Janan frowned at the young man before saying, "Well, Gregor, what is your tale? Where are those you came with? You surely did not make this trip on your own."

He was studying her less than spotless buckskins. A small frown was on his face. He glanced at Sallee, then back at Janan, before saying, "I wanted to follow Dains, but two bands came off the plain before I could sneak away." His study of Janan continued. The frown deepened. "Our leader, Lamoa, started the whole bunch on your trail right away. The scouts stopped when they found your totem, but Lamoa talked them into going on. Your cats chewed up the scouts some, but the main group got there in time to run them off. Lamoa sent the wounded back to camp, but the warriors were getting spooked. I heard some whispering about Dains sending her cats to stop us. When they lost your track sign there was more and more talk about Dains. I figure they didn't want to see the sign. Anyway, water began to get low, and they decided to turn back. Lamoa was fit to be tied, but without the other tribes she didn't have enough men. When they turned back I found a bush to hide behind."

Janan studied him a while before saying, "So you trailed us?"

The young man shrugged. "Until I lost my way. But I figured you were headed west, so I just kept walking. I had a half-full water skin, but it soon played out, as was I when I finally saw the hills."

"Well," Janan's smooth forehead was lined with a delicate frown, "I don't think we can let you return to your people."

"I don't want to go back!"

"Oh?"

"My family is no more, and they treat me like a servant, almost like a slave."

After a further study of the frowning countenance of the young man, Janan ducked out of the tent, where Mathou had listened to the conversation. Looking at the old man, she raised her brows in question.

He shrugged his shoulders. "Just as well. We don't want him taking tales of this land back to his tribe. When he is up and about we'll see what he knows about weapons, then see what he knows of wood lore, if anything. Keep him busy, and keep an eye on him."

Janan nodded. "Meantime, Carl and I will go check in with Da and find out what has been going on in the wood and on the plain. You might want to come along and check out our old village site."

"Nay, girl. I am not yet up to a long walk, and I don't want to make a track through the wildwood. I'll send a couple of likely lads with you to check out the village. Tell Jube that I figger we will spend a season here watching for any sign of trouble from the tribes and getting our animals back in shape." Mathou cracked a little grin. "And the same for our people. When I am in shape to travel without that blasted pony cart I'll come have a look. If you need to leave a message, put it in that cave where Megan stored things."

Janan chuckled. "Meg thought that was a secret. She should have known better; Jube and you both knew about it."

Jokome was checking his horses' hooves while tea water heated, when the riders arrived. He straightened to walk to the side of his wagon before hailing the five men.

"Heyla. King's men, aren't you? I hope you are not here to tell me that there are bandits about." The troop officer seemed a bit too senior to be leading a five-squad.

"Greetings, trader. No bandits that we know of. We look for an old trader and an escapee the king wants to talk to. The old man wore black and had an old black hat. We did not think he could have traveled this far unless he pushed his horses hard." The officer was looking at Jokome's team, but Jokome had wiped them with a wet rag as well as given them a good curry combing. Both were dry and without sweat signs, and both were placidly munching a ration of grain.

Jokome shook his head. "I have seen no other traders as I had hoped. I wanted company through the wood. I came on the trace from the east and spent some time at the camping place just below the junction. I suppose someone could have been ahead of me. But I forget my manners. Why don't you climb down and rest awhile? Tea will be ready shortly, and I have the fixings for a trail stew that cooks up quick."

Before long Jokome had served tea to his "guests," where they sprawled on the grassy verge of the trace. The senior soldier had declined the stew, not wanting to stop that long. But as all sipped the scalding brew, the officer returned to the subject of those he sought.

"The escapee we seek is a young woman wearing leather. She carries a sword and a couple of knives. We thought she might have come this way and had joined or captured the old trader to make him push his horses hard."

Jokome sipped from his cup of tea, then shook his head. "Not a soul on the trace. Couldn't you follow his wagon tracks?"

"Nay, as you might have noticed it has been a long dry-spell. The track of wagons and animals are many and blurred."

When the officer stood, his men followed suit. Then the officer frowned and said, "Traders are about as thick as thieves. Are you sure you have not seen another trader?"

"I am an honest trader, sir. I may be new to this area, but I know who rules. I know who not to cross."

The officer turned to his men. "Lenderson, you and Coss check out the wagon." He turned back to Jokome, an evil smile on his face. "Maybe if we put your feet in the fire you might have a better recall."

Jokome backed to the side of his wagon, reached under the wagon seat, and pulled out a big two-handed sword. "Nay, captain, this you will not do." He swung the sword, and the sheath slid off the blade. Then he took a stance and hefted the sword. "I am an honest man, but I know how to defend myself."

The five soldiers drew, then moved apart to give them sword room. Silence held as all appraised the situation. Then the silence was shattered.

"So, Gortson, you still like long odds on your side!"

The five shifted away from Jokome and backed a few paces away from the warrior who faced them with drawn knife and sword. The captain's eyes opened in surprise, then he scowled.

"Zackoro!"

"Aye, Zackoro, who you, Quintson and Antore left on the field of battle to die of my wounds. Without reason you deserted a fellow soldier; therefore, I call soldiers' justice on the three of you. I will start with you. You other men, stay out of this. It is soldiers' justice."

The captain's eyes narrowed. "Nay, men. Pay no attention to his ranting. Spread out. He is just one man. We will take him down."

"Two men." Jokome strode to Zackoro's side to take a couple of practice swings with his huge sword.

Zack glanced at him. "Can you use that thing?"

"Aye, an old warrior from the lands to the south of the sea taught me."

Zackoro eyed the five soldiers. "Well, men, will you back that coward and go against soldiers' justice? I fight for that justice, and this stranger will fight to keep you from torturing him. I think the two of us just might do a lot of damage before we go down."

"Make it three to five, Zack." A slender, buckskin-clad figure stood out from the verge of the trace, sword and knife in hand.

"Now it's four to five." Another of her like had joined the first leather-clad figure. "Hey, there is my pretty soldier. Don't kill him, Dee."

The young soldier, Ivor Lenderson, stared. Backing away, he yelled, "Look out, she is a witch. She has made two of herself!" Zack didn't like it, but couldn't do anything about the situation; he was about to find out how well he had taught the girls.

The captain lost his head and attacked Zack, galvanizing two others to try and flank Jokome. That was their first mistake. The huge sword in Jokome's hands was deadly as it swept down on the first man. He lost his sword to the big blade. It continued on, to slice into his thigh. The trader jumped back in time to block the blade of the second man.

As Jokome was backing his second attacker toward the wagon, Zack and his opponent were engaged in a furious and nearly equal duel. Behind these battles the two younger soldiers were finding that the two young ladies were their equals in blade work, if not size.

As it happened, Dee was facing the stunned young soldier, Ivor.

How could a young girl give him such a fight? As he battled the lightning-quick blade of her sword, she cheated. In a quick blur her left arm came around, and the young man had a knife in the biceps of his sword arm. As he reached with his left hand for his dropped blade, Dee heard Lee yell, "Don't kill him, he's mine."

With a commendable quick wit, Dee laid the flat of her blade along the side of his head. When he dropped like a pole-axed steer, she turned to where her sister was in trouble, and backed from her opponent. Without a thought for fair play, Dee stepped in and ran her sword through the man's sword arm.

Lee's sword point came up to rest in the pit at the base of his throat. "Drop your knife." Her voice was chill.

Dee turned, her sword ready, but it was over. Zack's opponent lay dead. Both of Jokome's were badly wounded and down. Her sister had hers backed up against the wagon and was suggesting that he sit before she decided to cut his throat. The one she had clubbed was still out. Of their four, only Zack had a wound, a cut in his side.

Lee was almost dancing in place. "What-a we do now!"

Zack grimaced, holding a bandage to his side. "Simmer down, youngster. The first thing you do is find some rope and tie their hands. Trader, you keep that giant's toothpick handy until the girls get them tied and have relieved them of any hidden weapons. Then we patch everyone up."

"Them too!"

"Everyone, Lee. A good soldier does not kill the enemy's wounded."

After Lee had used a fiery liquor to clean Zack's wound, she bandaged it, then moved to the warrior Dee had pole-axed. She first cleaned and bandaged his wounded arm, then began cleaning the cut on his head, using the same stuff she had used on Zack. The young fighter came awake with a yell. The liquor really did have a fiery sting to it.

"Hold still, stupid, till I get this cleaned out!"

The young soldier shook his head and blinked his eyes rapidly, trying to clear his vision. Lee had tied just his feet so he had his one good arm free to fend her off. "Get away from me, witch! What are you doing to me? Trying to poison my wound?"

Dee and Jokome had finished binding the wounds of the other three, so she wandered over to look at the young soldier trying to fight off Lee's ministrations. "What's his problem?"

"Oh, he's acting stupid. I think you hit him too hard. He won't let me clean his head, and he says I am trying to poison him. And he keeps calling me a witch."

"Yi!" The young soldier had a wild look in his eye. "You doubled yourself again, the better to torture me! Get away! Get away!"

"What seems to be the problem?" Zack stood looking at the three young people.

"Ah." Dee shook her head. "I think I thumped his head too hard."

"Keep her away from me! Keep her away. She is trying to put a hex on me!"

Zack held his expression with difficulty. "You two get out of here. Go help that trader catch the horses we spooked. I will take care of this lad's head wound, and watch the others."

"Whatever," Lee said. Then, before she stood, she put a hand on each of her patient's cheeks to hold him for the kiss she planted on his mouth. As Lee's patient tried to fight her off, Zack couldn't stop the chuckle that burst forth.

Fifteen

"Lenderson, you are the least wounded, so I count on you to get these men home." After a night of rest and a couple of meals, all the wounded, except the youngest, were mounted and tied in their saddles. Zackoro was instructing the young soldier before assisting him to mount. "I suspect you had better not stop on the way, or you might not get everyone back in the saddle. Just keep going. These men are in need of the ministrations of your troop healer."

Lee had snuck up on the pair and, as Zack prepared to help Lenderson into the saddle, she grabbed him around the neck and planted another kiss on his mouth.

As the young soldier fought her off, she said, "When you are all healed up you can come back and marry me, Ivor." Zack fought his laughter as he hauled her away and boosted the young man into the saddle.

Zack turned to the other solders. "All of you stay in the saddle at all cost until you get back to your troop. Lenderson is hale enough to get down and fill your water skins. Tell your troop captain that Captain Zackoro has called soldiers' justice on High Captain Quintson and King Antore for leaving a wounded comrade to die on the battlefield without reason."

As the horses began moving, Lee grinned up at Ivor. Face shining, she said, "Don't you forget me, you hear?" The young soldier's expression was one of horror as he kicked his horse into motion.

The four at the wagon watched the riders leave, with a lead horse bearing a grisly, blanket-wrapped burden. When distance and heat haze blotted out the sight of the riders, the trader turned to Zack. "Come on over here by the wagon. I will wash that wound with soap and water. After that I think I better use a little numbweed salve and put in a few stitches."

When the surgery was completed, and the wound poulticed and re-wrapped, Zack nodded his thanks and said, "Well done, stranger. You seem to have many hidden talents."

Dee giggled. With eyes shining with mischief she said, "Hey, Zack, Jokome isn't a stranger."

Zackoro's brows shot up. "Jokome!"

Dee's eyes were still shining, "Aye, didn't he clean up pretty? Wait till Ma sees him."

Jokome frowned at her, then grabbed her and turned her over his knee. Four good, hard whacks preceded his dumping her on the ground. While Dee glared and rubbed her bottom, he turned to Lee. "And you are next if you don't keep a civil tongue in your head."

While Lee danced out of reach, Zack was laughing so hard he had to hold his wound. Jokome frowned halfheartedly. "Careful you don't pull out the stitches," he grumbled.

When Zackoro got his breath back, he was holding his side and grimacing with pain. But the trader had prepared for when the effects of the numbweed wore off. After he had poured boiling water over the botanical in a small pot, he let them steep for a while before dipping out a cupful of the result. He gave the cup to Zack, saying, "Best you drink it down fast. It's bitter, but it will take care of the pain. The rest you can take with you. It works cold or hot."

While he waited for the pain to recede, Zackoro discussed their situation with Jokome. "Tell me, what brought all this on?"

After the trader had told the story of his and the twins' troubles, Zack eyed the girls with a look that spoke of more trouble to come. He then turned back to Jokome. "Where we go, you can't take your wagon. We will stay the night and send you off on the morrow."

"Well," the trader looked thoughtful, "I hate for you to take any chances, especially after what you did for me. If I were on the plain I would travel at night, but the wood is dark as a tar pit at night. I will move out now and use the rest of the day for travel; I won't stop until dark. If I keep on at that pace I should be in the south kingdom before anyone can catch up with me."

Zack nodded. "And we will stay near here for a day. If the girls go get their bows I think we can slow a small troop down before we have to disappear." Frowning, he said, "You won't be able to come back to the plain. They will be watching for you in both your guises. What will you do?"

"No big problem. I will work my route as far north as I can, without leaving the southern kingdom. I can keep track of what happens up here by listening to the traders' tales."

"Very well, and we will meet what traders we can to garner any news." Zackoro frowned. "If we want to send you word, what guise do we send it to?"

Jokome chuckled and eyed the girls, then, with a glint in his eye, he said, "I think I will stick with this one, but the name will be the same down there. Also, I think I will be far enough ahead of anyone that may be following, so that they won't catch up. Girls, you get him to Megan as soon as you can. No arguments, Zack. That wound needs taking care of."

Janan had the four of her party well separated as they moved through the wildwood. They were moving at a leisurely pace when the cry of a hovering hawk came from her left, followed by the call of a tiny barn owl.

When they had pulled back and gathered, Janan waited for an explanation. She knew Carl had not issued the warning; his bird calls were much better than those she had heard. One of their two villagers leaned in and whispered, "A camp fire, just ahead."

She nodded, then whispered back, "All right, we will separate ten lengths and creep up on the camp. Slow and quiet, with weapons at ready; let's go."

As they moved, Janan listened for any unusual noise, including any from her band of skulkers. She checked all around and up; men could hide in the trees. With nothing unusual to slow them, they came to the verge of a small clearing and an empty camp.

"You be a noisy bunch."

Janan whirled and found Jube leaning on his spear. "And you need some work on yer bird signals."

She chuckled, then told the two young villagers who stood with their boar spears poised, "Ease off, lads, it's me da."

Jube's fresh meat had been added to the trail stew mix the foursome had brought with them, making a good meal for the group. Jube's fire-cooked maize bread and tea added to that meal.

Janan had just finished the tale of her and Carl's travels. "Well, girl, for no longer than you were gone, sounds like you had quite a time of it. Glad you brought old Mathou and Sallee with you. It will be good to see the two of them."

"Mathou is wondering about rebuilding the old village, Da. He is wondering what Antore is up to."

Jube snorted, then said, "He has not bothered, since you last stirred him up. He doesn't even bother with a scout troop down this way." He raised his brows. "You said the villagers be a bit more warlike now?"

"Aye, and it would take a lot of soldiers to push them out of that village again." She chuckled. "And there would be a lot of dead soldier-boys if they did."

Jube grunted, then said, "Well, these two lads can come with us and have a look, then take a report back to Mathou."

"He said that they would spend a season where they are, Da, to rest up and watch that the plains tribes didn't follow."

Zackoro was lying out on a pad, letting the sun dry his wound, when he heard Jube's whistle signal. Minna went with Megan to open the gate, and he watched the warm welcome given the three that came through the prickly tunnel.

When Jube came trudging up to where he lay, he looked Zack over, then said, "How did you manage that?"

The answer came from Meg. "He tangled with some of Antore's men." She glanced at her recumbent patient. "That is enough sun, for now. Jube, give him a hand up and we'll find some shade, water and a bite. While we are rustling up that bite, Zack can tell his tale."

When they had settled in the shade before Jube's hut, Zack began his tale. "Well, Jube, when I brought in the meat I found the twins had gone to the cave. They told Meg they would go hunting if things were quiet. When the meat was smoked and packed in the cool cave I decided I better go check on the girls. When I got to the wood end of the cave I went up to hide my lamp and found the girls had left their bows and quivers in the slit. There was a trader wagon just coming to the wood and, way off, I could see a troop of horses coming down the trace. I slipped down to see what I could see, and…"

"End of story, Jube. The twins went to town, got in trouble, and Jokome had to pull them out. When Jokome was about to have trouble with the king's men, me and the girls pulled him out of it. You should see that giant's toothpick he was swinging."

"Where are the girls?" The glint in Janan's gray eyes bode nothing good for the twins.

"In your hut." Zack's grin was wry. "I locked up all their buckskins and weapons, and they have been sulking ever since."

Her brows shot up. "And what are they wearing, just their underclothes?"

Zack's grin was full-blown. "Some things Dee picked up in Kingston."

"Leeta! Deeta! Get your butts out here!" Janan's yell echoed around the valley walls, disturbing the goats. After a short wait the twins emerged from their hut and, while Jube snorted laughter, slowly made their way to the sunshade before Jube's hut.

Janan's brows were once again arched. Barefoot, each wore an embroidered gown. Their thick blond hair was combed smooth and fell down each back, almost to their narrow waists. From each side a hank of hair had been drawn to the middle of the hair flow, to be joined, holding the hair from spreading out. Janan was stunned. They were beautiful.

As the twins walked, slowly, to stand before their mother, Janan managed to get her surprise hidden. She had known the girls were pretty, but nothing had prepared her for this.

"So, for gowns you have caused Zack to be wounded. For adventure, you risk your own lives. For gowns, you risk Jokome and cause him to lose a good trade route. Very well, you may wear your gowns until I decide you have ceased acting like willful children. No weapons, no leathers, no boots."

"Aw, Ma, we didn't do anything wrong. How were we to know we shouldn't go up there? We just wanted to see the place and buy a few things Jokome didn't carry. 'Sides, I didn't want any old gown. I was looking at a good knife when those soldiers showed up. It was Dee who was buying those gowns."

"You knew it was wrong, Lee, or you would have asked one of your elders before you headed up the trace. And I suspect you were the leader in this little foray. Now back to your hut. We will have a meeting in the plaza tonight, and you will tell us of your journey. You will tell me about each step you took."

Back in their hut, the twins made tea, then sat looking downhearted. Dee was the first to speak. "I should never have let you talk me into going up there."

"Don't give me any of that cow flop. You wanted to go as bad as I did. 'Sides, I never heard any of the old folk say anything about not going up there." Lee took a big sip of tea, then grumbled, "Now we gotta drag around in these rags. We can't even go hunting."

Back at Jube's hut, while the meal was in progress, Janan told the tale of her and Carl's trip. When all had reached the point of leaning back with after-meal tea, Jube tilted his head to one side and came back to the transgressions of the twins. "I don't rightly remember anyone telling the girls they would be in danger in Dog Town." He raised one eyebrow to look at each of the others. "Did any of you say anything?" When no one answered, he continued. "Looks like us just figgered they knew what we knew."

Janan sat with delicate frown lines on her smooth forehead before finally saying, "I still think they knew better." Then she sighed, shook her head and said, "How long have they been restricted to their hut?"

Megan chuckled before answering, "Two seven-days."

That night, after the travelers had a good nap, all gathered around the fire pit in the "village plaza." When all had a mug of strong tea before them, Janan started the girls on their tale. She had not exaggerated about wanting to know each step each of the girls had taken. Lee didn't even get a chuckle when she told of the thieves running from the "marsh walkers." Dee did get a chuckle out of Jube and Zack when she said, "Well, Zack didn't recognize Jokome either. You remember what I told Jokome about his beard, hair and clothing, Grandpa? Well, I was right. He did clean up pretty."

At the end of the girls' tale, Janan was frowning. "Well, I heard nothing to change my mind. You two did a very stupid thing, so you just go back to your hut and consider just how stupid. Now git!"

When the girls had gone, she had a mild frown on her face. "Da, we had better go clean out the cave. Make sure everything is out of the slit and that there is nothing to show we have been there. The bones may scare any searchers out, but we can't chance it. Antore knows about Lee and Zackoro, and we sent him four wounded and one dead. He will send searchers." She gave a frosty grin. "But I don't look to see him leaving his castle."

"Aye, and we better send Carl back to warn our people to stay put."

Janan's eyes twinkled as she said, "I don't think that will make Carl too unhappy." Carl's face reddened as eyebrows around the fire went up, and more when Janan continued, "and I think Liddy will be glad to see him."

Jube managed a straight face as he said, "Liddy? I don't remember any Liddy. Whose be she?"

"Young Mark married Minda. Liddy is theirs." Janan's eyes sparkled, "And Liddy was very picky until your son showed up. She has been staying fairly close to Carl ever since he arrived on the scene."

In their hut the girls heard laughter. Peeking through the doorway, they were just in time to see Carl stalking off into the darkness.

The next morning Jube drew a map showing Carl the other route out of the Desolation. "This will bring you out in the wilderness about a two-day journey to the west of the old village site. That should keep you clear of Antore's men." He started Janan to chuckling when he added, "Now if you should get carried away, you can tell Mark and Minda that Jube approves of the match." Not knowing whether to be pleased or angry, Carl was again blushing as he went to collect his gear.

When Carl had gone, Janan led the twins to Zack's hut, where she presented them with their confiscated clothing and weapons. "You don't deserve to have these for another half year, but things are stirring." She frowned at the pair. "I think you two had better be armed. Just remember this: one wrong step, and you will not leave this valley for a year."

Janan and Jube left that night for the cave, hoping to arrive at the end that overlooked the beginning of the plain by daylight.

Sixteen

Carl met two of the village scouts a day's journey from the semi-permanent camp of villagers. He gave warning of the off chance that some of Antore's scouts might come their way.

That night the villagers sat around the fire at the center of the temporary village square while Carl told of the adventures of the twins. The tale of the marsh walkers brought a chuckle from the listeners, as it had not from Jube's group.

At the end of the tale, Carl passed Jube's message. "You had better stay put here, Mathou, 'cause those stupid girls have probably riled up Antore. Jube said that someone would come tell you when things have lightened up. I cannot stay long, because they may need me."

Mathou nodded, a frown on his face. "I think we had better extend our scouting another day's march and be sure our weapons are at full inventory." Then his features lightened. "And I think you should stay for a few days rest, Carl. We may need you to answer a few more questions, and Liddy might have a question or two." Mathou's eyes were sparkling as Carl's face reddened, then he said, "One thing for sure, I want to meet those girls of Janan's. It sounds like they take after their mother. Jan was a bit of a hoyden at an even younger age than you are now."

It was all of a moon later when Carl came through the prickly tunnel. After a meal he appropriated the hammock that swung from the trees by the cooling spring. When he woke, he had company. The twins were seated by the spring, gloomily contemplating the flowing water.

"Well, why the long faces? Is sis threatening to make you wear those gowns again?"

"Oh, shut up!"

"Not funny."

The first had to be Lee, so the second, less-forceful rejoinder had to have come from Dee.

"So what is wrong?"

Dee shrugged. "Ma is still sniping at us every chance she gets, and she won't let us stand guard together."

"So what are you guarding?"

"The caves. We stay way back from the far end and just listen. We have heard voices a few times, but no one comes very far into the cave. Zack and Grandpa heard some of them talking. Zack said they were loafing and drinking wine, and it seems that Antore sent a large party all the way to the southern boarder. Anyway, after that, things quieted down."

"So why the long faces?"

"Ma won't let us out of the valley! We can't even go hunting."

Lee looked up and made a face. "Said that if we even tried we would be wearing those gowns for a year."

"Hey, that wouldn't be so bad; you looked really good in them."

"Oh, shut up!"

"Aw, come on girls. She will get over it, and we may soon have a village. About a moon from now Mathou wants to meet with Jube in that old cave of Ma's."

That night they gathered around the fire pit in their "village plaza" while Carl told of his trip. "Mathou has scouts out a two-day walk east of the camp, and he wants you to meet him at Ma's dry cave about a moon from now, Da."

"Well, it will be good to see the old fool, and that will give us a moon to chance a lookabout. From what those layabouts who were loafing in

115

our cave had to say, Antore got word that we are all in the south kingdom. I suspect that Jokome might have had a hand in that."

The girls brightened, but their mother quickly put a damper on that. "No! You girls are not going."

And Jube did the same to Janan. "Nor are you, Jan. I will be the one to snoop around. In our bunch, Carl and meself are the only ones they are not lookin' for. I'll take a few small nuggets with me, no coin, and see if we can find out what is going on in the world. That is, if Antore's men have really given up on us."

Jube relaxed and gave his son a tiny grin. "Now then, from what you didn't say, I guess I did not gain me a daughter-in-law."

Carl reddened a little. "Not yet, Da, but there have been promises made. Liddy and I decided to wait until we have a village to do it up right in."

Lee jumped right into the conversation. "Hey now, that's not fair. Carl is out and about finding himself a wife, and we are stuck here!"

Zack grinned at her. "What's this? I thought you had already picked out Ivor?"

Lee grinned back. "He didn't seem all that anxious the last time I saw him, but he is sure pretty."

"Pretty stupid," Dee growled.

Carl chuckled. "Where did you find him, Lee?"

"In Antore's throne room."

Janan scowled and, as Carl roared with laughter, growled, "I ought to chain you to a tree."

"Hello, the camp," Jube hailed the three traders from the trace. They were in a layover camp in the woods, well away from the plain. As they came to their feet, weapons in hand, he showed his empty hands. His spear was strapped to his back. "I come in peace, and I am alone."

One of the traders stepped forward and said, "If ye come in peace, be welcome."

Jube strode into the space inside the circled wagons and threw down a deerskin that held fresh meat. Slipping both his pack and bedroll, he leaned his spear against one of the wagons. "Here is fresh meat for the pot. I be Jube, a hunter, and I am glad to find traders again traveling the trace. I have need of a few things, and the king's men have made everyone to shy away from this area. I have just finished a scout of the wood from the plain to the southern border. Looks like they have finally left us in peace. If you don't mind, I would like your company this night, sharing pot and night fire."

Another of the traders nodded to Jube. "Never heard of a hunter wearing a sword, but I have heard your name, Jube. You are one of those who trade with Jokome."

"Aye, but I have not seen Jokome in an age. What has happened to him?"

The trader chuckled and said, "Jokome seems to think the king is wanting his hide, so he has been staying in the south. If I ran across you, he wanted me to deliver a message. He wanted to know how you fared and wants you to send him word when it is safe to meet you at your old village site."

Jube chuckled and accepted a cup of tea. "So, I am glad to hear from Old Thief. He and his da are friends from before Jokome was old enough to trade, and I was one of his first customers."

The trader gave him a quizzical look. "Why do you name him 'Old Thief'?"

Jube chuckled, then grinned as he said, "When the lad first started trading, he tried to look a lot older than he was. That was when I named him 'Old Thief.' Except that he no longer walks humped over, he still tries to look older than he is."

The trader joined in the grinning, saying, "Well, he gave all that up. When I saw him down south I didn't know him, and he had a time convincing me that he was Jokome. Now, let's get some of that meat in the pot. This whole trip I have been living on bully beef."

The traders were headed south, so the next morning Jube took the one who had brought Jokome's message aside. "When you see Jokome, would you tell him that I will be at the old village site about twenty days from now. Tell him that since Antore seems to have stopped his running about and tearing up things, we are thinking about rebuilding our village. If we do rebuild, that will give you traders a stopover and place to ply your trade."

***

When Jokome rode a saddle horse into the weed-grown village plaza, there was quite a crowd waiting to greet him. When he climbed from the saddle, he was met by Jube, Mathou, Megan and Janan. With them were twelve armed young men from the camp of the villagers.

Jube stood staring at the trader, a frown on his face, until Jokome grinned and said, "What is your problem, Jube? Just because you can no longer name me 'old thief' doesn't give you the right to ignore me."

Mathou stood with brows raised in question. "Jokome?" Janan and Megan just stared.

Finally Megan said, "Well, I would never have believed a trimmed beard, a haircut and a few bits of clothing would turn an old man into a young one."

The corners of Janan's mouth were twitching suspiciously, and her gray eyes were a-star as she said, "Well, now, Dee did say that you had cleaned up plumb pretty."

"Aye," Jokome, in return, had one brow raised. "She got her bottom dusted for her lip, and I told Lee that she would get the same if she didn't keep a civil tongue in her head."

That did it. Janan broke out in laughter, then said, "Dee didn't tell that part of the tale."

Jube finally gave the trader a rueful grin and said, "So you are Little Jo again."

"Not quite, Jube, unless you are still calling Janan a little girl.'"

The fire pit in the old village plaza had been cleaned out, and pots of stew and tea were shared by the seventeen hungry people. Over the after-meal tea, Jokome said, "How soon do you figure to rebuild and move your people into your new village, Mathou?"

"Well now, according to our calculations it should take at least two moons to get our wagons through the wildwood. Then we will have to set up a camp before we can start building. I would say about six moons to have a working village, but we will have need of goods before that. We have a list of all we will be needing, but we are a bit short of coin."

Jokome slowly shook his head. "I am not rich enough to stake a whole village. I will need at least some earnest money."

Mathou brought out a leather sack, untied the draw strings and dumped out a small pile of coins. Jokome made piles of five coins and weighed each pile on a small portable scale. Among the silvers there were just a few gold coins.

After reading the tendered list of goods, he said, "What coin you have will cover maybe a twentieth of what you have on this list, even if I sell at cost."

Jube tossed a heavy pouch to the trader. "Weigh this."

With raised brows, Jokome dumped a goodly pile of gold nuggets and coin from Jube's pouch. After weighing the gold, the trader nodded. "Be about half again what is needed, Jube."

Jube chuckled, then said, "If ye know a good moneychanger, put the extra out at interest. That should cover anything else we might need."

Mathou raised an inquiring brow at Jube, who shrugged and said, "Found a small pocket of nuggets in a stream, and I cannot think of a better use for my find. Gold will bring back my village, a home for my family. I may never find any more yellow, so I will need my village."

Jokome nodded. "With the amount you are buying, I can give you good prices, but I want two things." At Mathou's nod, he continued, "I want to be your only trader for the first year, and I want that old road cleaned out before the third moon from now. The horse I rode could get in here, but my wagon cannot."

Mathou frowned at the trader before saying, "And after that year?"

Jokome's gentle smile caused Janan to stare. "After that I think my prices will keep you my customers."

Jube gave a series of small nods and said, "Things seem to be working out, but I think my bunch will be keeping an eye on the plain. If any of Antore's men show up snoopin' around, we will let you know. Both of you."

Jokome's eyes were sparkling when he said, "And it will be good to sit in on some old-fashioned village plaza doings."

The next morning Jube, Janan and Megan traveled to the trace with the trader, where they said their farewells. Jube had the last word. "We will be looking for you three moons from now. We plan on helping with the rebuilding."

After leaving the trader, Jube's group scouted their way to the plain, then made their way to the cave labyrinth, where they spent a full day watching the plain for movement. Finally they made their way through the cave system to their little green valley.

Seventeen

"There is a new village in your southern territory, King Antore. It is located at the south end of the Desolation."

"Why do you bother me with news of a grubby little gathering of huts, trader? There was a village there before, during the war of liberation, but rather than greeting me as their liberator, they ran from me. This act of treason cost them their miserable little collection of huts. Perhaps these are newcomers, or just maybe the old villagers have come back. When I get around to it I will send a five-squad to instruct them in the ways of the kingdom."

"Majesty, the village trades with just one trader, though the building of shelters was completed near six moons past. Even though other traders use the village as a stopover, none can sell there."

Antore chuckled, then said, "So that is your problem. Another trader has made a deal with this village, cutting you out of the trading." He chuckled again, a cold sound. "I should have you whipped for bothering me with your nonsense."

"Nay, Majesty, I beg that you hear me out. When I lay over there, I listen to the children. Among the names I hear is one that is familiar. Zackoro!"

The king's eyes narrowed. "And did you, perhaps, hear other names? Perhaps Minna or Janan or Leeta?"

"Nay, Majesty, but I did hear one addressed as 'Mam Min.'"

"Very well, trader. You may wait in the room down the hall, the first door on the left."

When the trader had bowed his way out, the king nodded to the captain of the squad stationed in the throne room. "Send one man to keep our talkative friend company." Turning to High Captain Quintson, he said, "Give the trader enough gold to keep him looking and listening for us. Also, see if he can give you numbers. We may need to know how many men are in that village and what weapons they carry."

Lee and Dee were enjoying the village gathering. The younger set was on the east side of the plaza, back from the fire, where neither light nor shadow dominated. Laughter, giggles and the sound of an occasional slap gave proof that things were proceeding in a manner that was normal. Those girls not keeping company with some young man were seated in a group, chattering between the entertainment.

The twins were seated side by side, wearing their party dress. This meant that all weapons, except their belt knives, were in Janan's four-room hut. There were traders staying the night.

Lee received a nudge in the ribs. "Hey, sis, who's that boy on the other side of the fire?"

Lee squinted her eyes, then said, "You mean the one who looks kinda weird?"

"Uh-huh, I have seen him at sword practice, but he seems to move any time I try to get close to him."

"Why would he do that?"

"Sure beats me, sis, but you can see for yourself. When the traders have all gone we will be back sparring with the boys. Watch him then. Just watch him when I try to go talk with him."

"If he tries to stay away from you, why should you care? And, if you ask me, he still looks weird."

"Oh, I don't know, Lee. I don't think he looks weird, just a little bit different. Kinda pretty."

"Got your butt busted once for calling a man pretty, so you better watch it. Besides, he doesn't look pretty to me, just weird."

It was a few days later when Mathou received a visitor. "Ah, Carl, be welcome." He grinned at his young visitor. "That hut you are building looks a bit big for just two. When is the big day? Have you laid the wood for your first fire in the fireplace yet?"

Carl gave a weak grin. "Now don't you start, old granther. I am getting enough of that from my two nieces." His grin faded. "Liddy has been telling me things about one of the traders. He walks all over the village, trying to get people to look at his wares, but Lid says he also asks a lot of questions. He seems to be numbering the men in the village, and he spends a lot of time listening to the children. Also, where the other traders stay over just one night, this one always stays two. I set Gregor to watch him." He gave a tight smile. "Greg is a lot more suspicious than our bunch." The smile grew. "And he is a big bunch more sneaky. He is laying on that accent of his and playing the ignorant outlander."

"And he seems to be a bit fascinated by blond hair, Carl."

"Aye, and scared to death of my elderly sister." He chuckled. "So much so that he stands back and stares at the twins, but is afraid to go close to them."

"Gregor is not yet convinced that Janan is not Dains, and that would make the girls daughters of a goddess. Sallee and I have tried to talk him out of this belief, but," Mathou shrugged, then said, "as for that trader, I have had my eye on him. We keep most of our weapons put away when he is with us. As far as that goes, we keep most hidden when any traders are here, especially the swords Jokome has brought us."

"Speaking of those blades, they are a lot more sword than those we have been using. Jokome told Da that the smiths south of the sea have a way of folding the blades as they make them, whatever that means."

Again Mathou shrugged. "All I know is that they take a keen edge and keep it for long, even at the pells. Gregor knows blades, and even he can't believe the quality."

Carl matched his shrug. "Zack says the same and is well pleased with the way the village men are taking to the sword. Even Greg has joined in the lessons. He says our swordplay is well above that of the tribe he came from. He says that it is no wonder that his tribe's leader was disarmed so easy."

"I am glad you came by, Carl. You have given me an idea. Gregor has been learning woodscraft from me, but I think I will ask Jube to take over that teaching. After a seven-day in the wildwood that old duffer can turn their campfire talk to Janan. I wonder what the boy will say when Jube tells him that Janan is his daughter and that the girls are his granddaughters?"

The next day, when Mathou sought out Jube and explained his problem, Jube chuckled and said, "Been watchin' the girls try to corner him and not havin' much luck. OK, I will take him in hand. A gaggle of traders is due to pass through, so the swordplay will be on hold for a while. Jan, Meg and the girls are heading back to our holding to check the livestock, so me and Zack will be at loose ends. Zack needs some rest, so I'll just take him along. Besides, he could use a little lessoning in wood lore, himself."

***

"Quintson."

The high captain bowed. "Majesty."

"I think it is time to look in on our new village. From what the trader says, the only weapons are a few spears, but I doubt not that there are a few bows for hunting. Since you know Zackoro and the three women, I want you to take a double five-squad and instruct our new subjects in their duties to the crown. While there, you and your men can look the situation over."

The high captain again bowed. "Very well, Majesty. As soon as the citywide celebration of your coronation anniversary and the last day parade of your army is over I will head south. Eight men and their officers should be sufficient."

The camp stew and pones of maize bread were a happy memory, and the after-dinner tea was a welcome relaxation. The conversation had gone past the next day's return to the village and had turned to the sword practice of the village men.

Zackoro sipped his tea, then said, "Jube, those women of yours are still better than the village men. They might even be better than Gregor here, and he has used the sword for years."

"Well, Greg had to unlearn some of what he learned from his people. They use a short sword and seem to use it more like a club." Jube turned to the young man in question. "That right, boy?"

Having grown used to the two older men, Gregor grinned at the old woodsman. "Not that bad, old man, but I must admit to believing I could outdo any in my tribe now. As for your girls, I don't know who you mean. There are just three women at sword practice. And they mostly teach the village girls."

Jube lifted one brow. "And you stay well away from all three, so…you'd not be knowin' that the older woman is my daughter or that the other two be me granddaughters, would you?"

"But, but, but…"

"Now, boy, you have it in your head that Janan be some kind of a goddess, but…if that be true I would have to be some kind of a god! Do I really look like a god to you? Drink your tea and think about it, lad, while I stoke me pipe."

When Jube had his pipe going, Gregor said, "But they don't look like the others."

Jube gave a series of small nods. "Aye, my first wife was from down south and had fire-red hair. Janan had her hair until she was about ten, then it began to turn. Finally it got to be a red-gold like it is now. Her daughters are another tale entirely. Janan's grandma had yellow hair, and the girls might have got something from their sire. Not many know that tale, but I will tell it to you so you will know."

Jube ended his tale with, "Now, do you really think a goddess would have let herself be raped? I don't think so, and I would appreciate it if you didn't repeat what I have told you."

While Gregor sat thinking, Zackoro dipped tea for all three, and Jube recharged his pipe.

After a long while the young man straightened, took more tea, then said, "So they are this Antore's daughters?"

"No, lad, they be Janandottir, and Antore is a marked man. If he comes near, Janan will kill him…or I will."

Anything but immune to the twins' good looks, when the three arrived back at the village, Gregor was looking everywhere for them while the two older men talked to Mathou.

In answer to Jube's question, the reluctant village leader said, "I was wondering about them yesterday. Wherever your lay-up is, they must still be there. Meg told Sallee that they might stay a couple of seven-days, said they had been neglecting things, and that they planned to do some repair work."

Jube turned to Zackoro and said, "Guess we better go give them a hand, or the ladies could be there a whole moon. Will Min be going along with us?"

Zack shook his head. "Don't think so. She won't want to drag Erick all that way."

Half-grown boys stood a two-hour watch on the road leading to the village. About halfway down the road, each boy in turn sat on a low limb within sight of the road's junction with the trace, watching for traders. This day the boy saw soldiers turning on to the road, and ran for the village square.

"How many?" Mathou asked the panting boy.

"'Bout ten or fifteen, on horses."

Mathou frowned, then said to the villagers who crowded around, "All right, men with boar spears and knives, women and children in the huts. Girls, get your bows ready, but don't come out unless I call for you or we are attacked. Now, everybody, move!"

When the small force of soldiers arrived, they found themselves outnumbered, but thought themselves better armed and better trained. The two junior officers kept glancing around for any hidden trouble. Should any trouble come up the road from the trace, the two men they had left down the road would sound the alarm.

High Captain Quintson rode his horse forward, looked over the force arrayed against him, and said, "We are soldiers of King Antore the First. We have come to see who has moved into his realm and to number them. You will call forth all who live here, and you will put down your arms. Who is headman here?"

Mathou stepped out, and Quintson saw an old man who was anything but feeble. "I guess I am, and we know of Antore and of his pillage and rapine. It was he who overran our village and destroyed it. Since that time we have had to learn to defend ourselves."

"King Antore!"

Mathou snorted and said, "So the brigand has named himself king? Well, that doesn't make him any less a brigand."

The high captain narrowed his eyes. "If I must bring the army down here, I will."

"If you do you may overrun us, but there will be a lot of dead soldier-boys lying around. We will pull back into the wildwood where your horses cannot go. Your bones will lie in the deep woods for the animals to gnaw on. Perhaps the day will come when we will accept the kingdom, but not while Antore's fat bottom rests on the throne." Mathou gave a thin smile. "Nor will Antore risk his precious hide down here. He will send you," he waved a hand at the mounted men, "to take a boar spear in your guts."

By this time the mounted men were looking worriedly around the village buildings, the thick woodland, and at the big boulder at the northern side of the village. "You will regret this day, old man." The high captain's rage was almost palpable as he fingered the hilt of his sword.

Mathou's voice was chill as he answered, "And you will regret it more if you make the mistake of doing what you are thinking of doing."

The senior soldier finally regained control of his emotions and spoke in a cold voice. "Very well, old man. I came to offer you the peace and protection of the kingdom. I will take your answer to King Antore." The horsemen backed their mounts to the edge of the wood, then wheeled and rode back toward the trace.

When they had gone, Mathou said, "Send scouts to the northeast to be sure they keep going."

About that time, children, who had been out foraging for fruit and roots, ran from the wood, screaming. One of the older girls ran to Mathou. "There were men on the road and Mam Minna told us to run into the wood." Women flooded from the huts, seeking their children;

two were missing, then a young boy came running up the road, yelling.

When Mathou finally managed to get the crying boy calmed down enough to talk, he shocked the listeners. "There were two men on the road, riding horses. When we came out of the wood they caught me and Jenny and Mam Minna, then a whole bunch of men came. They put Mam Minna and Jenny on a horse and rode off with them. A man told me that they would cut Mam Minna and Jenny's throat if they were attacked."

Eighteen

It was midday when Carl met Jube, Zackoro and the women. He was just a league into the Desolation. The first thing he said was, "Zack, Minna has been taken by the king's men." His quick explanation sent the whole group into their ground-covering lope.

It was early afternoon when they arrived in the village. They found organized chaos. Mathou was organizing a pursuit band.

Zackoro stood listening to Mathou and Jube talk between the orders the old man was giving. Finally he had heard enough. His shout overrode all else. "Everybody shut up!"

Captain Zackoro used his parade ground bellow, which drew a shocked silence. He quickly pointed out ten men, Jube and Mathou, "You come with me, now! The rest of you continue your preparations." The twins and Janan followed, unasked; Carl and Gregor trailed along behind.

Walking to the cold fire pit in the middle of the village plaza, Zackoro told those he had called forth to take a seat. Taking in the sight of the extras, he frowned, but said nothing.

"Now all of you listen to me. You know next to nothing of warfare, so I am taking command. And no, you don't have any choice in the matter." He took a stance, the heel of his hand resting on his sword hilt.

"First, there is no way you can follow that band into Kingston, let alone into Antore's castle. Jokome, Lee and Dee have all told you of that place, and I know it well. You go against that walled city and you get slaughtered."

When low grumbling started it was cut off by Zackoro's raised hand. "I have long thought of an assault on that place, and have made many plans. The plan I came up with would need a small group of well-trained warriors, and I could not ask anyone to go on such a foray because I wanted justice for just myself. Now my wife and one of your children have been taken from us. I plan not a sword assault, but a dagger strike." He looked at the village men. "None of you have the skills needed."

Zackoro turned to Jube, who returned his gaze and gave a slight nod. Deliberately turning to Mathou, he said, "Whether you like it or not, you are the village leader." He looked at each of the other ten villagers in turn. "You men are the village's lead warriors, whether you know it or not. If my group succeeds and we come back down the trace I will need at least half of your men and half of the bow-trained young women waiting at the northern edge of the wood. You cannot leave the village undefended, so the other half of those trained for battle must stay here. If we are followed our band will not meet the soldiers head on; we will fade before them until all of our warriors are together."

With the villagers dismissed to their planning, Zackoro turned to Jube. "I think Megan is not going to like this."

Jube gave a small grin. "Aye, but we will leave that trouble for later." The grin disappeared. "You have a plan to lay hands on Antore?"

He nodded before saying, "Meg has repaired my captain's uniform, and that will get us to the main entrance to the castle. We can take out the two guards on duty, drop the portcullis and close and bar the doors. At dusk Antore meets with his high captains. They will be alone to keep the ordinary soldier from knowing what they say."

"How many total?"

"Just three; Antore and the two high captains. At times the chamberlain is also there."

"Three, maybe four." Janan arched one brow. "Sounds like I had better go along."

As Jube started shaking his head, Zack nodded once and said, "Your right is at least as strong as my call for soldiers' justice." Then he turned to the older man. "I know your thoughts, Jube, but she is right; we may need her." Jube held Janan's eye a long moment, then gave a sharp nod.

Zackoro turned to the group of youngsters. "As for you three, you will stay here in the village. If it comes to it I want you to join Meg and my son in our valley. The three of us will settle Meg and my boy in the valley, then we will head for Kingston." Trying to lighten the mood, he grinned at the fourth member of the younger group. "And you just as well take this barbarian with you. He might be of some use."

Gregor gave back grin for grin. "It might be a good way for me to figure out which of these wild women is which."

Ever serious, Carl said, "I will ask Liddy if she will go with Ma. That way Ma will have some company, and I won't have to worry about Lid. If we have to pull back into the wildwood we can take that other route you showed me, Da, and come to the valley that way."

Liddy was armed with knife, sword and bow when she left with those heading for that small green spot in the middle of the Desolation. They started out in the wood, but soon cut back to the Desolation. The idea was to keep the location of their valley a secret still.

Those bound for the valley had not been gone long when Jokome drove his wagon into the village. Not long after that he gathered with the twins and the two young men; he had decided to take a hand in the game.

The young people watched with fascination as the trader used shears to trim away his beard. The twins giggled when he soaped his face and began shaving with a small, sharp, funny-looking blade.

Finally finished, he was drying his face when Dee said, "Whee, Ma should see this!"

"Quiet, or I will dust your tail again." But his frown was not so fierce with a naked face. "Those idiots will need help getting into that city, and that means one of you will have to waylay them before they get on the plain. You tell them to go to the western side of the marsh, the fourth night from now, and wait. I will let down a rope for them to climb. Now, you say that there will be just three of them?"

"Aye, but me and Dee have been talking about that, and we think we ought to go with them. After all, we have been there before."

"If the girls decide to go along, I think I will tag along too." Gregor had a lopsided smile on his face. "I know the plains and can scout the route ahead of them."

"Zack said for us to stay here." Carl's frown tried for fierce. "If things go bad, someone must guard Ma and Lid."

"Aye, Uncle Carl." Lee's grin was impish. "I think that should be *your* job. After all, they are your women. Dee and I will look after Ma."

Carl turned away from the sight of Lee's fun-filled face. "I know why the girls are going, and I think I know why Greg wants to go, but why you, Jokome?"

The trader stood long moments, looking uncomfortable. Finally he said, "Jube and Janan are friends from long time back, and Jube and my da were close, as were Janan's ma and my ma." He scowled the frown that was now not so daunting. "Besides, if Antore is gone I can trade in peace in Kingston again."

It was tempting, but Lee kept her suspicions to herself. After all, she didn't want her bottom busted.

Turning to the twins, the ever-serious Carl again shook his head. "Sis won't let you go, but you three can take Jokome's message to them. After that you can introduce Greg to our valley."

Lee was looking rebellious when her sister turned her face away from her uncle, winked at her sister, and said, "Our child uncle is right, Lee. You know Ma, she thinks we are still little girls. At least we can take some fresh meat to Meg and Lid." She turned to the trader. "Are you stopping over at the campsite on the plain?"

"Yes, the horses will need rest. When I get there I will probably spend the night."

"Uh huh, so I guess we better let Ma know. She may want to slip in and talk to you."

"You think she and the others will be on the plain so soon, Dee?"

"Sure. They will probably be on the plain about as soon as you, and they will want to travel at night. The way we plan to travel will get us there before you. I just hope you will be the only trader there."

"It is probable that I will be alone. Most traders went early so they could be there for the celebration of Antore's throne-taking anniversary. Now you three had better get on your way if you plan to get there before me. I will be on my way as soon as I have a little talk with Mathou."

When the trader and Carl had walked off, Lee looked at Dee and asked, "What was that all about?"

The normally more conservative twin grinned, then shrugged. "I'll tell you as we go. Right now let's get our stuff and head out before Jokome has too long to think about what I said. Water bag, sword, knives, trail food and bow. You can shoot a bow, can't you, Greg?"

Gregor frowned, then asked, "Which one are you?"

He received a big grin with his answer. "Dee."

"Well, Deeta, I will contest you when we get back. Let's get going."

When they arrived in the cave overlooking the beginning of the plain, Janan climbed to the slit to hide their candle lanterns. There she found a strip of hide so big it could not be missed. The message on the hide was not signed. Jokome will stay the night on the plain. He shaved.

Zackoro frowned at the message, then at Jube and Janan. "We had better take this with us. It needs burning or burying somewhere. I wonder who left it."

Janan didn't wonder, and her language was not ladylike.

Jokome had just finished a big bowl of stew and was enjoying his tea and after-dinner pipe while wondering if he would need to throw out most of the big pot of stew he had cooked up. Evidently the three expected visitors were not going to show.

"Heyla, old thief." Jokome dropped both tea and pipe. "You got extra in that pot?"

He came to his feet with his two-handed "toothpick" in his hands. He was staring at his wagon, where the voice had come from.

"Careful with that thing, Little Jo."

Exasperated, he said, "Jube, I may strangle you. Come out here and get some stew."

Jube was chuckling. "I don't think so, we better stay out of the firelight."

As his eyes adjusted, Jokome finally made out three shadowy figures lying under the wagon. His lips had a wry twist when he said, "I have never served guests under my wagon before, but I guess there is room for you to sit up. I don't want to have to pour perfectly good stew and tea on the ground."

When each of the three had a bowl and mug, Jube handed him the written note and said, "This your work?"

Taking it to the fire where he could see to read, Jokome let loose a blistering curse, then threw the hide in the fire.

Janan said, "That's about what I thought. Where are they, Jokome?"

"Your guess is as good as mine, but mine says they are somewhere ahead of us."

"Is Carl with them?"

"No, but that barbarian boy is. Carl stayed with Mathou, but he told the girls to take my message to you. He also said that you would send them to stay with Megan."

"I will chain Leeta to a tree for a year!"

For a while only the muttering of the fire could be heard, then Jokome spoke up while shaking his head. "I think you have the wrong one this time, Janan. Leeta was about to blow up on Carl for saying that they could not go with you when Deeta quieted her and spoke of taking fresh meat to some valley." He shook his head again, then added, "And I thought Dee was the level-headed one of the two."

"Then I will chain the pair of them to a tree!"

Jube heaved a sigh. "Young they are, Jan, but they are also women grown. We will send them back if we can, but I have a feeling that they will be a part of this little foray."

While Jokome talked with Jube and Zackoro, Janan was brooding over the actions of the twins. She soon caught herself studying the trader's clean-shaven features. Dee was right, she decided, he is pretty.

Greg and the twins had used his open-country expertise to travel by both the light of the sun and the light from the moon. Now they lay under a large, thorny bush in the small wood just south of the city wall. All were staring across the open space between the wood and the wall.

"What's that smell?" Gregor wrinkled his nose.

Lee grinned while saying, "That is the marsh Jokome was talking about."

"Wheew, it sure stinks." He frowned at the imposing city wall. "How do we get over that wall? Wait for Jokome's rope?"

Lee shook her head. "Na, Ma would just send us home." She frowned for a few quiet moments, then said, "Dee, you remember those two that thought we were some kind of a spook?"

"Yeah, what about them?"

"Do you suppose they ever came back?"

"I dunno. Why?"

"What do you bet they don't go into the city through any of the gates? You think they might have another way in?"

It was Dee's turn to hesitate, then nod. "Aye, they didn't have the look of honest city folk, did they? Too bad we didn't bring those black cloaks; maybe we could have scared them into telling us how they get in."

"The moon's near half, Dee, and if we come along that ledge from both ends of the marsh maybe we can lay hands on them if they are there."

"Right, and as soon as it gets dark enough to move across that open space, we will split up. You take the west end, Lee, and I will take the east."

"Are you planning to leave me here?" Gregor was up on one elbow, shaking his head a little. "I don't think so, girls."

"Naw," Dee drawled, "you can come with me 'cause Lee don't think much of you. 'Sides, I might need help. Those two ran east when we spooked them before."

The thief was asleep on his straw pallet, and when the scuff of a boot on stone woke him, he tried to come to his feet. Three long blades

stopped his rise, then a sword point touched the back of his knife hand.
   "Drop it," said a quiet, feminine voice.

Nineteen

Minna stood as at attention in the throne room, holding Jenny's hand. Dusty, disheveled and tired, she stood with head high. Dignity was in her stance and on her features.

The king was aware of that dignity. "I am glad to welcome you and your child to my realm, Minna. Is she one of mine?"

Minna's nose came up slightly as she said, "Captain Zackoro has called soldiers' justice on you, Antore, for abandoning him on the battlefield without reason. Now you have kidnaped a soldier's wife, with rape on your mind. As for this child, she is not mine. Does Quintson now steal girl children for your pleasure?" She turned her head to look at the guards stationed in the throne room. "Soldiers, look to your wives and girl children if you have them."

Antore was furious but let nothing show on his face. A soldier's family was sacrosanct, and soldiers had been known to revolt if this tenet were violated. He could not let his guard leave the throne room thinking such a violation had occurred.

With a cold smile he answered the accusation. "If you are wife to ex-soldier Zackoro you are wife to a renegade. As such you will be held until he turns himself in or is captured. As for bedding you, I'd as soon bed a sow. Nor do I bed children." Turning to his chamberlain he said,

"Escort these females to my son's quarters. That should be both safe enough and comfortable enough for them, and probably much better than the pigsty they usually live in."

***

Two men and a woman sat in a clump of bushes, gazing through the heat haze at the distant city. Finally Janan untied the water skin from her belt, took a long drink and then said, "We just as well get some sleep; we can't approach the city until dark."

Jube reached for his water, saying, "Wonder where the girls are? We haven't seen hide nor hair of them since that all-clear sign."

"Are you sure that was what it was?" Zackoro asked before taking his drink.

Jube chuckled. "Aye, soldier boy, three four-stone cairns in a straight line and pointed in the direction they were traveling. The kids are good at hiding their tracks, but they know I can track them. I had forgotten about teaching them about that all clear marker. 'Twas before your time."

Janan's eyes still held an angry spark. "We should catch up with them at the wall. We'll check out that wall by the marsh, then pull back and wait for tomorrow night. We can start those blockheads back to the valley before daylight."

Jube grunted, then said, "So you can have the first watch. Wake me in four hours."

It was just at the gloaming, and a half-moon was just rising when the three started toward the city. They moved quietly, using any and all cover they could find. Coming to the small wood, well after dark, Jube motioned the others to cover while he approached the thin tract of trees. Shortly there came the cry of a nighthawk, and they moved to join him.

The night had advanced until it was well past midnight, and Zackoro was looking across the bare space between the wood and the wall. He reached for his knife when Janan touched his shoulder. Janan had scoured the wood to the west while Jube had gone east.

"Dammee, woman, you move too quiet," he whispered, "I almost had my knife in you!"

With an equal quiet, Jube appeared out of the night. "Found a camp past the marsh. They weren't hid, and they had a fire, so I guess they were honest folk."

"At a guess, there was no sign of the kids since neither of you mentioned them?"

"No," Jube whispered, "and I think it is time we try locating them." With that, he sent out his nighthawk cry. Shortly the cry of a screech owl came from the edge of the marsh. "That was Lee," he said. "Let's go."

They were right up against the wall when they heard three clicking sounds. Jube pulled his knife and, using just the tip of the blade, tapped the wall twice. A shadow detached from the shadow of the marsh reeds and approached. "Heyla," whispered Leeta.

The whispered answer came from her mother. "When I get time I am going to strangle you. Where are the others?"

"In the city. Come on, follow me before the patrol comes by or this stink kills us all."

"Now just one moment, young lady." It was too dim to see Zackoro's scowl, but it was in his voice, whisper or not. "Just where are you taking us?"

Lee was already moving when she answered. "We have a lay-up in the city." As she led them out on the ledge between the wall and the marsh, she added, "Get it moving and keep it quiet. 'Bout time for the watch patrol to come by."

They were well out in the marsh when Lee ducked down and the three followed her lead. As they waited, the three she led heard what had caused her action. From the south side of the marsh came the sounds of mounted riders. When the sounds faded to the west, Lee motioned them to follow. Shortly they came to a large, circular opening in the wall about waist high.

"This is a storm water runoff drain," Lee whispered, "and it can only be used when it has not rained for a while. I will go first. There is a bull's-eye candle lantern about twenty lengths in, but I can't shine it back this way. After about another twenty lengths this big drain ends where it is fed by a bunch of smaller drains, but there is a ladder that leads out of the drain. At the top of that ladder we will have room to stand, and there is a regular candle lamp we can light."

When they finally gathered in a rather wide, stone-walled passageway, Lee lit a candle lamp and blew out the bull's-eye to hang it on a hook driven into one wall. Then she said, "This is an old smuggler's route, but the smugglers have all been driven out of the city, or hung."

Janan, checking for mud, found very little on her hands and knees. Lee, seeing what her mother was doing, chuckled, then said, "A good rain usually ends up cleaning that drain pretty well, so our informant tells us."

"Informant?" Janan raised her brows.

"Aye, we caught one of those thieves that thought me and Dee were spooks. He was sound asleep on the ledge. We told him that we would not feed him to the marsh if he would show us how he and his friend found their way into the city. After we got settled in I came out to see if you would show up tonight. Dee said not, but I thought you might."

Starting to walk the up the sloping passage, Lee said, "Come on, we are almost there." The passage ended at a wood panel, and Lee tapped three times. A short wait and two taps answered her signal. When Lee slid the panel aside, Dee was facing them with a drawn sword. Across the small room Gregor stood near a seated stranger, sword in hand. The stranger's legs were tied to the stool he sat on.

When Janan started in on Dee, the stranger shushed her. Then, in a low voice, he said, "Keep it down. If someone hears you they might wonder where the voice is coming from."

Gregor gave her a grin. "Doubson says that this place is not too air tight. We are in a cellar below a hide storage warehouse. He said they quit using it for storage because the hides got moldy down here."

"Doubson!" Zackoro took Lee's candle lamp and walked over to the seated man. Holding the lamp near the face of the captive he said, "What are you doing here?"

The stranger squinted up at Zack, then said, "Captain Zackoro!" He frowned, then added, "We heard you were dead, then we heard you were alive and had called soldiers' justice on Quintson and Antore, after you had dispatched Gortson."

"You heard right, but what about you?"

"You probably wouldn't know, but I have a wife and son to feed. Well, when someone got careless about our pay I had to have money. Bribes from a smuggler band carried me through the lean times, but when someone turned us in I had to run. Now I feed my family as best I can. I have been trying to get enough gold and silver together to get them out of here and down south, but pickings have been slim." He shrugged, then grimaced. "I'm not a very good thief."

Zackoro slowly shook his head. "I thought Antore would have better sense than that; his soldiers keep him on his throne."

Again the ex-soldier shrugged. "After you put Gortson down, word got around that he was the one collecting our pay."

Zack snorted, then said, "Sounds like him." Turning to Gregor, he motioned to the prisoner. "Untie him." The young plainsman raised his brows but did as he was told.

After being released, the soldier-turned-thief stood and started stamping his feet. As he worked to get the circulation going, he frowned at the twins. "I told one of you that you were tying that rope too tight. If we'd have had to run for it, I probably couldn't have."

Lee grinned at him. "You didn't seem to have any trouble running when we met before. I really didn't have much hope we would find you on the ledge again."

"What are you babbling on about?"

"Look, sister, food for our pool." Lee's voice was a hoarse whisper.

"You were in those black robes!"

"They were just hooded cloaks."

The ex-soldier slowly shook his head, a wry, twisted grin on his face. "Well, you two cost me my mate. When he spooked I had to follow. Besides, I couldn't face two swords with just a knife. I tried to talk him into coming back, but he set off down the trace. He said he was going down south and find honest work."

Dee frowned at Zackoro. "You trust him?"

"Aye, he was in my band, and was a damned good soldier. I was thinking of promoting him just before I had my trouble."

Dee was still not satisfied. "But he is a thief."

141

Zackoro turned to the man in question. "Well, Doubson?"

Doubson held up his right hand. "Soldier's honor, captain."

Zack turned back to the suspicious girl. "Dee, you don't know, so you can't understand the soldiers' code. Just take my word for it; he is trustworthy." He turned again. "Do you have any of your equipment, Doub?"

The man's answer was to walk to a wall panel. He did something that caused a slight click, then he slid that panel aside. In the space behind the panel hung a uniform, a belt-hung sword and knife, and a pair of boots.

After closing the panel the ex-soldier opened another to bring out a table. It had legs that folded, and it was very sturdy. Another opening held eight stools and a metal contrivance of some kind. A wooden box held candles, tea, cups, and of all things, a teapot. The metal contrivance had mounts for six of the candles and a rack to support the teapot.

Doubson grinned and said. "Can't offer you a hot meal, but we can have tea."

"If you have all this, why sleep on that ledge?" Lee wanted to know.

The ex-soldier shrugged. "Don't use the drain in daylight, lest someone sees me. I made the mistake of oversleeping tonight."

Jube chuckled before saying, "Well, we can furnish the meal if you don't mind smoked deer jerky and cold corn dodgers."

The six candles boiled water in a surprisingly short time, and the meal was soon in progress. While the refilled pot sat reheating, Zackoro asked about watch movements, guard changes and many other things that went on in the city. Finally he asked, "Is there any chance of someone coming down here from the storage area up above."

Doubson shook his head. "The smugglers, years ago, sneaked up there and removed the trapdoor, then laid flooring boards over the hole. I doubt anyone even remembers this place now, and there is a door to the outside that looks like part of the outside wall."

While a second round of tea was being served, and more water was being heated, Doubson turned to stare at Zackoro. With disbelief in his voice he said, "You are going after Antore! That's why you are asking all these questions."

Zack studied the ex-soldier for a time, then nodded. "Aye, and you may want to take your wife and boy out of here. If we take out Antore this city could come apart."

"But…why? Surely not just for what he did to you. If you somehow manage to get to him, how will you get back out?"

"We have our plans. One of us escaped from the palace before, and we think we can use the same route if it became necessary. As for why, he has my wife and a child he stole from our village. We have come for them."

"You're mad!"

Zack grinned. "Not dead in the black, Doub, but close."

Twenty

In his black and hooded cloak, he was just one more shadow in the shadowed alley. Jokome waited until the four soldiers of the night patrol turned into another street, then darted into the side street they had come from. It would be another two hours before they returned. At the city wall he moved quietly west until he could overlook that end of the marsh. As he looked down the wall he could see nothing but shadows. With the tip of his knife he tapped the signal Jube had taught him. From behind him came two taps. Shifting his knife to his left hand as he turned, he swept his "toothpick" off his back.

"Easy with that thing, Little Jo." A shadow stirred, then Jube stepped into the moonlight. "Put that thing away and come along. We got a ways to go." Two more men joined Jube in the moonlight.

"Jube! How did you get up here?"

Jokome saw the white glint of teeth when the old man answered. "The twins found us a way in." When they joined him by the rail he saw Zackoro was one of the other two. The third man he didn't know.

Zack gripped his shoulder, then said, "Come along, trader. We have a lay-up, and we have to get to it without having a run-in with the patrol." He turned to the third man and said, "Lead off, Doub."

The way was long, but they finally stopped by the wall of a large building. By the smell, Jokome thought they must be near the tannery. They moved slowly down that wall until the stranger leading them seemed to find what he was looking for and rapped three times. The two taps came back, and a dark opening appeared. After all four had passed through the opening, something blocked off the moonlight that had followed them in. A bull's-eye lantern was unhooded. Gregor stood to one side, holding both sword and knife at ready while one of the twins held the light.

"I see you found him, Grandpa. Come on. I can't wait till Ma sees how pretty he is without that beard."

"Dee!" Jokome reached for her. "You're looking to get your butt busted again."

She dodged back. "Watch it! Don't make me drop the light." As she started down a narrow stair, she added, "Come on, there is hot tea waiting."

Soon Jokome, Jube and Zack sat facing the others. A lamp was between the two groups, but Janan sat back in the shadows staring at Jokome. She had seen him by firelight back on the plain, but with the lamp lighting his features clearly she was beginning to understand the twins' cheeky remarks. She had laughed at their calling him pretty when he had changed his looks the first time, but had not paid much attention to their nonsense this time.

All were listening to Zack with care, but Janan's agile mind could handle more than one thing at a time. She had always liked Jokome the trader, but now...she shook her head slightly, trying to see what the difference was.

Janan let Zack's words come into focus. He was summing up. "So that is about as far as we can plan. The three of us will take out the two guards, close the doors, then drop the portcullis. It will be some time before anyone wonders if something might be amiss, and even longer for them to decide to do something about it. That will give us plenty of time to do what we have to do. Doub, you and the kids can go out the tunnel and head for that wood down south. Jokome, I have seen traders towing carts behind their wagons. I believe you hire out to move families that way. You and Doubson can make arrangements to get his family out of the city, then he and the kids can meet you down the trace."

Lee stood to give him a sly grin. "Sounds good, Zack, 'cept the kids will be going with you."

Janan spoke up. "You will not!"

Lee shrugged. "How you gonna stop us, Ma? 'Sides, we told Carl we would look after you. Greg can go with the others, but you are going to need Dee and me."

Gregor, from where he sat, shrugged and said, "Six sounds like about the right size for this little dagger strike of yours."

The situation tickled Jube's sense of humor, so he said, "What makes you want to join our little frolic?"

The young barbarian gave him a small grin and an equally small shrug. "Figure I better go along and make sure that loudmouth Lee's sister makes it back to the village in good enough shape to marry me."

Even in the lamplight, Dee's red face stood out as Lee said, "I told you he is pretty strange."

Finally interrupting the fun and games, and Janan's smoldering, low volume tirades at the twins, Jokome stood. "Just about what I figured, so I brought equipment for seven." He reached behind him and dragged his pack within reach.

As he hauled ropes and black and hooded cloaks out of the pack, Janan decided she knew what it was that was so different about the trader. His dark brown trousers, shirt and jerkin looked like a uniform. With the baldric-hung sword on his back, and wearing both a boot knife and belt knife, he just didn't look like a trader. An inner voice said, "The girls are right. He is pretty. Well, handsome, really." She was so surprised by the thought that she quit arguing with the kids.

Jube just looked at the twins, shrugged, grunted, then said, "Figures." He then turned to the trader. "How do you figure we will need gear for seven?"

Jokome shrugged. "Thought I might go along."

Zackoro came to grip his shoulder. "The thought is appreciated, but you are needed to help Doubson and his family, and to vouch for them to the village folk."

Jokome frowned at him, then said, "You might need me to help you get out of the city. How are you planning to do that, and how do you get out of the castle?"

Zack gave him a sly smile. "You have already taken care of that. Soon as I saw those extra ropes you brought I thought of how Lee and Dee got out of the city the first time, and it looks like you did too. Right now my problem is how to get *into* the castle."

Jokome's face went blank for a while, then he said, "You know, I just might have an idea for that. I brought those cloaks to make your group less noticeable, but they give me another idea now." After a hesitation, he continued. "It would not be all that unusual for a religious order to come to the castle with a petition to open a temple near the city. In this instance the black robes would signify the Crone. Carl said Janan has had practice at playing goddess, so playing priestess should give her no trouble."

It was time for Zackoro to be thoughtful for a time. Then he said, "I was thinking of having Gregor put on Doubson's uniform and help me escort prisoners up to the castle gate. They are about the same size and shape, but this could work out better. Let's take a long look at this thing."

The next morning Jokome had moved his wagon farther uptown and had turned it around. While he was attaching a two-wheel cart to the back of the wagon, Doubson's wife and son were carrying their pitifully few possessions to a pile by the cart. The cart was almost loaded when a contingent of the guard walked up.

"Trader, you look about ready to leave the city. Do you go south?"

Jokome kept a neutral face as he answered. "Aye, and I also transport this good widow south to her family."

The sergeant in charge said, "Good, I think you may just be what the king is looking for. Come along."

"A moment please, sergeant. Do you know what this is all about?"

"Not for me to say, but I guess it wouldn't hurt to tell you that I think he has another passenger for you. You just come along now. The king will tell you all you need to know."

Jokome glanced at the horses to be sure they were well tied, then he spoke to the boy standing with his mother. "Water the horses, lad." To the boy's mother Jokome said, "I will be back as soon as I may. Be sure your cart is well packed and ready to go."

As he walked with the guard contingent, Jokome was worried. He was fair caught if someone had turned him in, but the guard seemed at ease as he traded city gossip with them. When they arrived at the big entrance to the castle the two on guard there waved them on through the big double-door entrance.

When they arrived in the throne room they had to wait. The king was going through a ritual with each of five men. Three soldiers of the regular army, and two of the city guard, were receiving an advancement in rank. Finally telling the five off to stand with the five-squad on duty in the throne room, Antore waved Jokome and his escort forward.

After receiving their bows, Antore said, "So, sergeant, what have you brought me?" The king was lounging on his throne, sipping a glass of cooled wine.

The sergeant bowed again before answering. "Sire, I have found a trader who is headed south, and he is giving transport to a widow and her young son."

The king turned his gaze on Jokome. "And how far south do you go, trader?"

Jokome bowed. "Majesty, I go to the southern kingdom."

"And you trade as you go?"

"Yes, Majesty, when and where I may."

Antore was well pleased. With so many of the army and of the guard in the room, the tale of what he did would spread fast. The trader was clean and clean shaven, and since he was transporting a widow and her child he would be considered trustworthy.

"Are you familiar with the village at the south end of the Desolation?"

Jokome bowed as he answered. "Aye, Majesty, I do a fair amount of trade there. They are not overly prosperous, but it is worth my time to stop by."

"Well, would you mind delivering another passenger there for me. A little girl from that village was accidentally brought in with a prisoner, and I would like her returned to them."

It was with relief Jokome bowed once more. "Your wish is my command, Majesty. It is quite probable that she will know me. I get along well with the children of that village. A bit of sweet goes a long way with those childings."

Antore turned to his chamberlain. "Bring the girl and a gold piece for her transportation."

When Jenny arrived it was with noticeable reluctance she was towed in by the elderly chamberlain. She appeared frightened, with her face streaked with dried tears. The old man towed her to the trader and dropped her hand, then turned to place a small gold coin in his hand.

Jokome gripped the coin tight in his fist and turned to the king. With apparent reluctance he said, "Majesty, payment is unnecessary. I am well pleased to carry out your wish, and the villagers will think well of me."

Antore chuckled. "And that will be good for trade, eh?" He then waved one hand in an airy gesture. "Keep it, trader. I treat fairly with my subjects and guests. Just see that the girl is safely returned to the mother." Turning to the guard sergeant who had brought the trader to him, he said, "Escort them out of the castle."

Jokome took the girl's hand and said, "Do the king a courtesy, child." He then bowed toward the throne. After a hesitation, the girl gave Antore a small curtsy.

They were halfway across the plaza that fronted the palace, and the girl was trying to free her hand from Jokome's grip, when he smiled down on her. "Now let me see. I think your name is Jenny, and I will wager you don't know old Jokome the trader without his beard, do you?" The girl quit struggling and stared up at him, so he added, "And your ma is Sarah, isn't she?"

The girl nodded but kept silent, so Jokome gently asked about Minna and about where the two of them had been kept. All the way back to the wagon she kept peeping up at his face and away. When they arrived at the wagon, Mam Doubson descended on the girl with little cries of dismay. Leading her to the cart, the good wife found a pan, water and a cloth to wash away the tear stains. As she worked she caught Jokome's eye and gave a slight nod toward a very narrow and dimly lit alley.

Taking the hint, the trader walked over to lean against the wall by the alley. In a quiet voice he asked, "Who?"

"Doubson. What's going on? The wife said the patrol came for you."

"Tell the others that Antore hired me to take Jenny back to the village. We will be leaving soon. You will find us stopping for the night at the camping place halfway to the wood." After passing on what he had learned from Jenny, Jokome pushed away from the wall to stroll to the wagon and begin the final preparations for the trip.

"He did *what?*"

Doubson had to grin when he answered the open-mouthed Janan. "Antore hired the trader to transport this Jenny back to her village."

Zackoro frowned while Janan was speechless, then said, "I would give a lot to know the why-fors of all this, but this will be a help to us. I figured we would have to take turns carrying the girl."

Doubson shrugged, then said, "She look to be about the same age as my boy, and the wife was already tending her. Jokome also said to tell you that the girl, a boy and your wife were all held in some kind of a fancy dungeon."

Twenty-one

The boy was talking to his friend, whose cell was down the passageway and across from their quarters. "How is it, Ivor?"

Faintly Minna heard the reply. "Not so good, Al. My wounds have finally healed, but my face is hot. It's all that witch's fault. If she hadn't kissed me I wouldn't be in this mess. That kiss was a jinx spell!"

"Anything you need, Ivor?"

"Water. I am so thirsty. And food. Al, you wouldn't believe how skinny I am. It's all her fault. She makes two of herself and fights like a man. Both of her fight like men." He mumbled curses and more words. Finally even that trailed off into a senseless jumble.

The boy kept calling, but finally even the mumbling stopped.

Minna sighed, then said, "I think he is asleep again, Almon. He needs good food and a healer, and he needs to be out of here. It is a wonder that all of us are not down with that same fever. For all that our quarters are by comparison luxurious."

Almon slumped down in a chair and said, "He doesn't deserve to be down here. He did nothing wrong." Dejected, he slumped lower, and Jenny walked over to pat his hand in sympathy. When he took her hand in his, he smiled at her and spoke quietly—Minna again thought him aged beyond his years.

"And here is another that should not be here. None of you should be here! If only I had been quicker with my knife!"

The sound of the iron bolt that locked the door to their prison sliding back brought the youngster to his feet. The heavy door swung open to reveal the two hulking, cowhide-clad keepers of the dungeons. They stepped in to take up a position on either side of the opening, staves held at ready.

The chamberlain followed them in. Before he could speak, Almon said, "Kemoc, Ivor needs to be taken to the army healers. He is dying, Kemoc. He doesn't deserve to be down here anyway. Can't you do something? Talk to High Captain Alberson. He is a decent man."

His face without expression, the old man finally nodded. "I will try." Then he walked over to where Jenny was hiding behind Minna and, seizing her hand, drew her toward the doorway. When Minna tried to interfere, one of the hulks pushed her back with his stave. When Almon leaped after the girl, he did not fair so well; a well-placed stave end punched him in the stomach. He doubled over, then fell to the floor.

The door closed and the bolt shot home. Minna stood staring at the grill in the door, listening to Jenny cry. The chamberlain's face appeared behind the grill. "The words you spoke in the throne room have born fruit, Mam Minna. The king is sending the girl home. He does this to placate the soldiers. There is a trader who is also transporting a widow and her young son who will deliver her to her home village." Then the chamberlain was gone.

When the sounds of Jenny's sobs faded, Minna turned to the boy. He was lying in the fetal position, holding his middle and trying to get his breath back.

"Are you all right, Almon?"

He heaved a big sigh and said, "I think I'll be sore for a while."

Minna helped him off the floor and to his bed. As he lay there, massaging his stomach, he said, "Well, I tried. You don't suppose he would really…"

"You didn't hear what Kemoc said to me?"

"I guess I was a little distracted at the time. What did he say?"

When Minna had told him the chamberlain's words he narrowed his eyes, then said, "Do you think we can believe him? And what did you say when you were in the throne room?"

After Minna had explained, the youngster was quiet for a time. Then he said, "Aye, he is that sly; maybe it was the truth. Now I can just hope that Kemoc will speak to Alberson."

The two soldiers on duty at the entrance to the castle watched a small group of dark-clad figures move across the plaza below to begin the climb to the stone-floored space before the wide doorway. When they arrived the guards drew their swords, and the senior soldier called for them to halt.

All four wore black and hooded cloaks that hid all but their faces. The gloom from the late afternoon shadow made the faces indistinct, but the one in the lead was a woman.

The senior soldier looked at the face of the woman with his squinted eyes. "State your business, woman."

"We are here with a petition. We wish to petition King Antore for permission to locate a temple near his city, a temple that will be dedicated to the worship of the Crone."

"You waste your time, woman. We worship the one God. Your heathen goddess is not wanted here. If you bother King Antore with your heathen nonsense he will probably have you whipped out of the city, if he will see you at all."

The soldier gave a shiver when a clawed hand emerged from the woman's cloak, and a hissing voice said, "Have care, man. She likes not to be insulted."

Just then a captain of a soldier band brushed by the women, followed by his aide. "What is going on here!"

The two saluted, then the senior guard said, "These foul old women claim to want to petition the king for a temple dedicated to some heathen goddess, captain."

The captain frowned at the women, saying, "Return at sun high tomorrow, then the king may consent to see you." He then turned to the guards. "The sun is low. Come along, it is time to secure the castle."

The soldiers were a bit puzzled by the orders, but were not about to argue with a captain. Sheathing their swords, they followed the captain and his aide through the doorway. They did not notice the silent, black figures following right behind them.

When all had disappeared into the relative dark within the castle, there came a sound of scuffling and a few grunts, then all was silent again. Shortly the aide came back out and pulled first one then the other huge door closed. Then came the sound of the three large bars dropping in place. A few moments later the portcullis rattled down. The iron extensions dropped into the holes bored into the rock floor on either side.

Just within the castle, two slightly battered, trussed-up soldiers glared at their captors over their gags. The "captain" had just come back down the stair he had climbed to get to the portcullis locks. When they had shed their cloaks, the four women turned out to be one woman, two girls and an old man. All were armed to the teeth.

The captain walked over to look down at the two wrapped in rope. "Men, I am Captain Zackoro and, if you have not already heard, I have called soldiers' justice on Antore and Quintson. Without reason they deserted me on the battlefield, leaving me to die of wounds I received in battle. They have since stolen my wife, a soldier's wife. You have done nothing wrong, you followed the orders of an army captain and were overpowered by six well-trained warriors. Believe me, there is not one in my band who could not match you with knife, sword, spear or bow. There is no shame in your capture. If you do not give them reason, those I leave here on guard will not harm you."

Zackoro turned to assess his little band. Then, with a nod, he said, "Jube, will you and Gregor stand watch here. We want no harm to come to anyone other than those we seek, but these doors must stay closed."

When Jube had nodded, Zack turned to the twins. "The two of you will come with your mother and me. You will stay in the hall outside the throne room. You will watch that no one comes up behind us and, keeping out of sight, watch the throne room too. You will be our bowmen." The girls grinned at that but said nothing. As Jokome had found out, they knew when to be serious.

He turned back to Jube. "If it looks like someone is about to break in, run toward the throne room. You know how to drop and lock the portcullis now, and there are four of them between here and the end of the hall."

"So, Kemoc, who is this prisoner you wish to remove to the army healers." The king had a slight frown on his face as he tried to remember if there was a soldier in the dungeons.

"His name is Ivor Lenderson, Majesty. He was with Captain Gortson and was wounded in that fight."

"Oh, yes, he was the one consorting with little Leeta."

"Aye, Majesty, and he named her a witch. He claimed she made a duplicate of herself to help with the defeat of a five-squad."

Antore chuckled. "Yes, I would say the girl had a bit of witchery about her." He chuckled again. "Aye, and she attempted to put a spell on him when she was here in the throne room. It all comes back to me now. I put him in the dungeon for coming up with that stupid excuse he used to excuse his defeat by a young girl, and for being ignorant enough to believe in witches. Very well, Kemoc. You may bring him before me, and we will see if he has learned anything."

"That would not be advisable, Majesty. He has a fever."

"Thank you, Kemoc. You are quite correct in not bringing a possible pestilence into our presence. After we are through here, see that he is taken to the army healers." Antore turned to the third party in the room. "Now, Quintson, what is your plan for that village that caused you to turn tail and run?"

High Captain Quintson had a burn across his cheeks as he answered. "I will take ten bands of foot and four bands of horse, sire. Half the foot will go south of the village, then circle to the west and set up to receive them when they try to fade into the wildwood. I will then come at them from the east."

"I don't think so, Quintson." Zackoro and Janan stood in the doorway.

The king didn't hesitate, and at his call two hulking soldiers came from behind a wall hanging. Each was swinging a spiked mace. From right and left they tried to close on Zackoro, ignoring the woman. The one on the left realized his mistake when Janan's blade took off the hand holding the mace. Then she turned the stroke and took out his throat. Zack dodged the mace of the warrior on the right and drew his sword blade across the mace swinger's stomach. When the mace dropped to the floor as the warrior clutched his middle, Zack's blade split his skull.

Zackoro wrenched his blade free just in time to meet the rush of High Captain Quintson. When he had beat down the attack, he gave his opponent a cold smile. "So we were expected, coward. Well, justice is now at hand. Defend yourself."

Janan had turned toward the throne, her sword at ready, but Antore had not moved. She lowered her sword and said, "You are armed, Whoreson. Defend yourself. Either way, you die."

Antore smiled. "So, little Janan, you have come to take revenge." Not turning his head, he said, "Kill her, then reload for the other one."

To one side of the throne one of the hangings was thrust aside, and Antore's fat eunuch stood there raising a boar crossbow to his shoulder. Before the stock of the weapon hit his shoulder, an arrow buried its self in the right side of his chest, then a second arrow hit the other side. As he crumpled, the bolt from the crossbow flew wild.

As she turned from the sight of the falling eunuch, Janan was moving toward the throne, raising her sword to ready. Antore was staring at her, transfixed. The bolt from the crossbow had entered just behind his left arm, and its point had emerged from the center of his chest.

Antore's attempt at a smile was a grimace, then he said, "Too late, little one." Blood flooded from his mouth as he rolled forward out of the throne.

Janan quickly turned to the other battle, but it was over. Zackoro was leaning on his sword, panting. She looked into his face and saw it lined with pain. "Are you all right, Zack?"

"Just a few nicks to bandage. What happened to Antore?"

From the hall outside the throne room came a young, feminine voice. "Oh, no you don't, old man. Stay put or I pin feathers on you." The chamberlain had been edging toward the hangings to the left of the throne. All was static until those hangings were thrown aside; a man wearing the uniform of a high captain stood there.

The newcomer's quick glance took in the situation, and he drew sword. Zack's voice brought the newcomer's head around. "Put it away, man. You don't stand a chance."

The fatigued and bloodstained captain leaned over to clean his blade on his vanquished opponent's clothing, then he sheathed the weapon. While the newcomer watched through narrowed eyes, Janan walked over to one of the mace swingers and cleaned her blade. Sheathing her sword, she walked over to the watcher. "Put it away. Our bowmen are looking at you down their arrows right now, and their arm might get tired."

His blade was still bared when the man said, "It is obvious that you have killed the king and his high captain. Why?"

"I am Captain Zackoro, and I had claimed soldiers' justice on Antore and Quintson. Janan Jubedottir had a prior justice claim on Antore, so she was to face him. My only regret is for the common soldiers."

"There are two more of them out here, Zack," one of the twins spoke from the hall, "and they had those funny-looking spiked ball thingies too."

When the two "bowmen" stepped through the doorway, the newcomer was startled by the sight of the two very young and very feminine "bowmen." He noted that, though they had lowered their bows, the arrows were still nocked.

Janan glanced their way and said, "Lee, run check with your grandpa. Don't tarry, hurry back." Then she turned back to their visitor. "Now, then…"

When she hesitated, he furnished a name. "I am High Captain Alberson, and I would very much like to know what happened here in sequence."

"Well, in a nut shell, high captain, we came here to get Zack's wife out of Antore's clutches and to take justice on him and Quintson. When we faced them, Antore called those mace swingers down on us. We took them out, and Quintson tried to backstab Zack, but Zack was too quick for him. While they did battle, I challenged Dog Antore. He wouldn't face me, but called in that eunuch of his and told him to kill me with his crossbow. The girls feathered the eunuch. His bolt flew wild, and Antore got in the way of it. Now, do you put that blade away or do I take it away from you?" Jan was tired and cranky.

The old soldier had the temerity to smile, then he sheathed his blade and said, "I do believe you would have tried. It might have been interesting. I have never crossed blades with a woman."

Janan just grunted and looked cross before bullying Zackoro into sitting on the throne. While she checked and dressed his wounds, she kept a wary eye on the two older men in the room.

While the older soldier walked the room to study each body, the chamberlain kept edging toward the hangings. Finally Dee said, "You, old man, go stand in the middle of the room. You move one more time and I feather your ass."

Her mother said, "Watch your mouth, Dee!"

Lee returned with word from Jube. "Nothing is moving, Ma, anywhere on the other side of the doors."

High Captain Alberson stood looking at the people standing around the room. "That won't last. The guard changes at midnight." Then he looked around the room, again and shook his head. "One man, a woman, two girls and a grandfather storm Antore's castle and succeed in taking it."

He was still shaking his head when Zack gave him a little grin. "One more; a barbarian boy."

Alberson snorted, then said, "Don't mourn those dead soldiers. They were prison scum Antore trained up after you put Gortson down, captain." He then turned to the chamberlain. "Where is this man's wife?"

"She is lodged with the boy."

"Well, go get her and the boy. No!" Alberson grew a small frown. "I think we had better go with you; I had forgotten those keepers."

Twenty-two

Zack, his face blank, stared at High Captain Alberson. His eyes narrowed. "You seem to be taking all this in stride, high captain. I wonder what is going on in your mind?"

The older officer's smile was thin. "This had to happen one day. Antore never got over being a warlord, and he was a poor king. And no, captain, despite what you may be thinking, I have no desire to be king." He nodded in the direction of the chamberlain. "But Kemoc and I now have a problem. How do we hold this kingdom together? If, when all this comes out, we have rioting in the streets, the kingdom could fall apart. Since the two of us are all that is left of the king's advisors, we must find a way to hold it all together."

It was quiet for long moments, then Zackoro said, "Aye, and there is the rub. Since you were advisors to Antore, I cannot trust you."

Again the thin smile. "Then we must find a way to build that trust, since for all intents and purposes you hold the kingdom. Come along. We will free your wife and introduce you to Antore's son. He shares his quarters with the captain's wife."

Janan started back, blinked and said, "Antore's son!"

The old warrior's smile was warmer. "Yes, battle maid, a son."

Janan relaxed just a little and smiled back, saying, "Since our

159

bowmen are my daughters, you better make that 'woman warrior,' you old war horse."

"The boy is in the dungeons because he tried to knife his father. He thought Antore had poisoned his mother." The old soldier slowly shook his head. "How he got this notion in his head, I don't know. Antore will answer to the one God for many things, but not for the death of the boy's mother. She died of a fever, which spoiled Antore's plans for the boy. Antore married the woman, intending to formalize making her his consort at a later date. The boy is a prince of the realm."

"How many soldiers man this castle?" Zack had not lost his suspicions.

"Antore depended on his prison scum. They knew if something happened to the king they could not run fast enough to escape the noose. Other than the guards at the entrance there are just the two keepers of the dungeons."

"Soldiers' honor?"

"Soldiers' honor, Captain Zackoro."

"Very well, High Captain Alberson, lead the way, please."

The senior officer walked to the wall hangings to the left of the throne and pulled them aside, revealing a large door. Janan took the draperies out of his hand and yanked them from the wall, then watched as he worked the complicated latch. With the door open, Alberson led the way, Zack right behind him, sword in hand.

The old soldier took note of the twins right behind Zack, arrows still nocked. Janan followed the chamberlain, and when the door started to close on its own, she pulled over a heavy chair to block its closing. As she caught up with the others, she too drew sword.

They walked down a long, wide hallway until the chamberlain called a halt and yanked a bell pull. Janan was at his side immediately. "What was that for?"

"There is one other in the dungeon, and for him we will need the castle healer."

"And just who is this 'one other'?"

"One whom I believe some of you might know, one Ivor Lenderson."

"What!" yelled Lee. "What's he doing down there?"

"It seems that he was consorting with the enemy, someone named Leeta." The old man kept a straight face, but his eyes were twinkling. "He also had the temerity to name this Leeta a witch, using this as an excuse for being overmatched by a young girl."

An older woman came into the hall as Dee said, "I told you he was pretty stupid."

The woman walked up to the chamberlain, her passive face belying the curiosity in her eyes. When she had curtsied, the old man said, "Anna, please inform the castle healer that he is needed in the dungeons and that he will need his two helpers and a stretcher."

Zackoro held the older officer's eyes for a long moment. "Just how many people are in this castle?"

"All is well, Captain Zackoro. Including the healer and his helpers, there is a total of twenty-three servitors. There will be no interference with your plans; come along."

While they walked toward the big door at the end of the hall, Lee questioned the chamberlain. "What's wrong with Ivor?"

"Starvation and fever. I had just secured permission to remove him to the army healers when I was interrupted by a group of rude women warriors."

"I may kill someone!"

"Lee!"

"All right, Ma. I'll keep my temper…for now."

To open the heavy door to the dungeons three big bars had to be lifted out of their brackets, and then a portcullis had to be raised before they could start down a wide set of stairs. It was dank and gloomy long before they reached the passageway at the bottom of the stair. When the leather-clad keepers came charging up the passage, Dee and Lee stepped to either side of the group to draw their bows.

The chamberlain threw up his arms. "Stop!" Recognizing the old man, the keepers slid to a stop and stared at the girls while he continued. "There are two reasons for the two of you to start running. The first is that one of the young ladies holding those bows is quite interested in the prisoner in the far cell. Second, the king is dead, and the boy will soon be King. I suggest that you run for the northern border and hope that you are not found by anyone who has spent time down here."

The pair had started backing as he spoke, and turned to run before he finished talking. Lee, while watching them run, said to the old man, "Sounds like those are the ones I should have killed."

Almon and Minna heard the approaching noise and had backed to the rear of their cell when the door opened to allow for Zack's entrance. Minna stood still, frozen for a long moment, then she ran across the cell to throw herself into his waiting arms.

The boy stood staring at the chamberlain who had followed Zack. Finally he said, "What is this, Kemoc?"

"You are free, Prince Almon."

"Prince!"

"Yes. Please come with us and all will be explained."

"What about Ivor?"

"The healer and his helpers are removing him from his cell."

Almon ran through the doorway only to find a buckskin-clad young lady kneeling by Ivor's stretcher. She had a bow in one hand and was holding her other hand to Ivor's forehead. When he knelt down across from the girl, she glanced at him and frowned.

Ignoring the girl, he gripped Ivor's shoulder and called to him. The ill soldier opened his eyes to look up at the face of his friend and mumble, "That you, Al? What's happening?"

"You are free, Ivor, and a healer is seeing to you."

"The fevered man's eyes wandered, only to lock on the face of the girl. "Look out, Al," he yelled as he thrashed about. "She is back, the witch! She'll put a hex on us."

"Pretty stupid." Almon looked up to see the duplicate of the buckskin-clad girl standing across the passageway, then the healer's helpers pushed him aside so they could strap the thrashing patient to the litter. Each to an end, they picked it up and started up the passageway. Lee and Almon walked with the patient.

The healer turned to shoo them away, saying, "I think this is just dungeon fever, but I would rather you two did not go with us. As soon as I am sure this is not a pestilence, you will be allowed to visit the patient."

Janan heard the healer and said, "Lee, get your butt back here. We can't get separated." Looking at the boy, she added, "Bring him with you."

When all had gathered back in the passage, Alberson turned to Zackoro, saying, "The keepers will have left two doors open, and each has its own portcullis. We had better secure those, then get back upstairs."

The raiding party would not stay in the private quarters of the castle, so the chamberlain ordered a meal brought to a room just off the hall leading to the main entrance to the castle. Zack made sure both the high captain and the old chamberlain ate with them. Finally the twins took food to Jube and Gregor. While the two ate they were brought up to date on what had happened, and Gregor grumbled that he was missing all the fun.

At the end of their tale, Jube nodded and said, "Tell yer ma that there are soldiers on the other side of these doors, and that we may need you to man the arrow slits above the doors."

On the twins' return, Dee passed on Jube's words and added, "Shouldn't we start thinking about getting out of here, Zack? Be getting light soon."

Before he could form an answer, Alberson caught his attention by saying, "I suppose you plan to take your leave the same way the girl did when she was here before?"

"We might, depending on how many soldiers are at the gate."

The older man nodded his understanding, then said, "It might be safer for you if you decided to stay for a while."

"Just what do you mean by that?" Janan growled.

"If this city comes apart, all sorts would be fleeing. The plain, the south wood, your village, would not be entirely safe. Now I have need of warriors I can trust to hold the castle until I can be sure I control the city. I can trust you because you have just two irons in the fire, the safety of those with you and of your village."

"And you think the seven of us, you, a boy and that old man can hold this place?" Zack had not lost his suspicion.

The high captain shrugged. "It will not be for long. If all goes well you will be honored guests of the future king. After all, he appears to believe your wife can do no wrong. If all does not go well we will all use Antore's bolt hole. I think I can control the army, and the army can assure order in the city, but we must move fast."

Zack looked at Janan, frowned and said, "If we go over the wall we will not have to worry about these two turning on us."

"Counting Minna and the boy, we would be ten." She glanced around the room and saw the boy was asleep, his head on Minna's lap. Then her gaze sharpened. "Where is Lee!"

"Here I am, Ma." The girl was just walking through the doorway.

"Where have you been?"

"To the throne room, Ma. The bodies are all gone, and there is a bunch of folk fixing and cleaning the place. I slipped over for a look below the balcony; there's a bunch of soldiers down there."

The chamberlain broke in. "I told Anna, the housekeeper, to have the dead taken to the dungeons, and to have the staff clean the throne room."

"Well done, Kemoc, now you should see to the body of the king." The high captain stood, then turned to Zack. "Someone has organized at least some of the troops. Time is not on our side, and we should go see who stands before the castle gates. You are too late, captain. You should have gone over the wall as soon as you had retrieved your wife."

Zack slowly nodded his head. "You are right. I took too much interest in things other than those I came for. Very well, High Captain Alberson, we will try your way. Remember, I will be watching and listening."

After waking the boy, they moved out of the room and walked toward the castle entrance. As they went the senior officer questioned Zack. "How many arrows have you, captain?"

"All of us brought a bow and full quiver. As I count it, four arrows have been expended."

From behind them came Lee's voice. "We retrieved them, Zack."

The high captain chuckled. "Well-trained they are." Then he turned his head and added, "Young lady, will you go on ahead and inform your grandfather that we are coming."

When they arrived at the gates, Jube, Lee and Gregor were spread across the passage. Each had a bow in hand, with an arrow nocked. The older soldier smiled when he saw them, then frowned when he saw the trussed-up soldiers.

"Untie them," he ordered.

No one moved until Janan said, "Gregor, loose them."

The men had to be helped to their feet before they could salute the high captain. He in turn said, "What kind of shape are you two in?"

The senior of the two answered, "They fed us and gave us water. As soon as we work out the kinks I think we will be all right, sir." The shamefaced man squirmed, then said, "But we need a trip to the guard room. There are relief stations in there."

The old soldier snorted, grinned, then said, "And while you are in there, get cleaned up. You will be backing me when we open these doors." His grin became a chuckle when they all but ran to the guard room.

Jube walked over to look the senior soldier up and down before saying, "Pretty fancy duds. You must be that high captain the girls told me about. Mind telling me what is going down?"

Alberson, in turn, saw a "grandfather" that looked as tough as many an old sergeant he had known. With a nod he said, "As soon as those two return from the jakes, we will work out our plan. We don't have time to dally."

"And you trust those two to do as you tell them?"

"Believe me, to the ordinary soldier a high captain is looked on as a god. They will follow orders."

"And why should we trust you?"

"Because your Captain Zackoro will have told your granddaughters to shoot me first, should anything go wrong."

Jube gave him an evil grin. "And they would, too."

Twenty-three

"How many soldiers are outside the doors?" High Captain Alberson stood in the wide entrance hallway, looking up where the twins and the young man of his ill-matched troop were manning the arrow slits over the big doors.

One of the girls turned and said, "There are two long lines of soldiers, one line down each side of the stair. Then there are four standing just outside, talking to each other."

The old soldier turned to the remaining members of his band and said, "Positions!"

With their bows in hand, Zack, Janan and Jube lined up across the hall; Minna and Almon removed to the guardroom. The two common soldiers raised the portcullis and lifted the bars off the big doors to lay them to one side. After settling sword belts and checking both sword and knife, they took up positions behind the high captain, a step back and to either side of the officer.

Alberson pushed one big door open and strode through the opening into bright early morning sunlight. The four officers just outside, from long habit, lined up and saluted.

"Good morning, gentlemen." The senior officer returned their salute before continuing. "I am glad you are here, but not overly proud of you forgetting your early training." Not expecting to be chided, the eyes of all four widened slightly as Alberson continued. "The arrow slits above the doors have been manned since your arrival. Senior officers do not risk stray arrows when commanding."

All four officers shifted uncomfortably as he continued talking to them. "The realm is in grave danger from within, and rumors may start making the rounds. Now, these are your orders: first you will go to your junior captains and tell them to take their five-squads and secure the city. Tell them that I do not want heavy-handed suppression, but there is to be absolutely no disorder of any kind; all commerce is to continue normally. After you are sure you have things well in hand, return here. You are invited to the throne room for a strategy discussion. Secrecy is the order of the day, so have your aides stand down to your offices until they are called for. That is all!"

All four officers saluted without hesitation, and turned to the stair. One officer shouted a staccato set of orders to those soldiers standing on the stair, then as the columns of soldiers began moving down the steps, the senior captains trotted down the stair between the moving men.

After the doors were again barred, Zack looked up at those manning the arrow slits. "What's going on down in the square?"

Gregor leaned over the walkway rail and said, "There is a lot of milling around, but the square is fast becoming empty."

Alberson nodded with satisfaction, then said, "So far so good, and all is prepared for our little show in the throne room." Turning to the two soldiers, he continued. "You men are once more charged with guarding the castle entrance." Turning, the old soldier pointed to the three above the doors. "These bowmen will be your backup. If just the four senior captains return, let them in. When they proceed to the throne room, bar the doors and drop and lock the portcullis. Your bowmen will then follow the captains to the throne room. You will remain on guard here."

When the four senior captains arrived at the doorway to the throne room, they saw an oddly dressed formation of warriors standing along the wall that faced the throne. After they had walked through the opening, more of these warriors followed them in. The high captain stood before the throne, and the chamberlain stood before the door that opened into the private regions of the castle.

Alberson waved to the several chairs before the throne. "Take a seat, gentlemen." As they moved to the chairs he spoke to the others in the room. "Wine for the captains, please."

Two girls, identical in every way, stepped forward. One carried a server covered with wine glasses, the other a wine pitcher. The first girl offered her tray to each captain in turn, letting them choose a glass. The second poured wine in their glasses, then they served the high captain. Finally two glasses were filled half full. Each girl took up a glass and drank off the contents. The tray and pitcher were placed on a table just down from the throne, then each girl retrieved the bow she had left leaning against the wall where the other warriors stood.

"Now, gentlemen, the proprieties have been observed, and you have wine for the coming ceremony." The senior officer turned and nodded to the chamberlain. "Commence the ceremony."

The chamberlain rapped on the door with the ornate staff he carried, and the door opened. A bier was carried into the throne room by four servants. On the bier lay King Antore in full formal array, even to the crown on his head. Just behind the bier walked a young boy. The boy wore formal robes, and a thin silver circlet crossed his forehead. Behind the boy walked a woman wearing robes of a less formal cut.

The four senior captains had come to their feet, staring, but the high captain soon caught their attention. "Soldiers and senior captains of the realm," Captain Alberson held his glass high, "the king is dead, long live the king."

The four hesitated, but finally took the required sip from their glasses. The high captain then turned to the boy. "Prince Almon, if you will, please take your place." The boy was helped by the woman to a seat on the throne; he sat on the front edge of the oversized seat, his feet not quite touching the floor.

Turning to the servants, the senior officer instructed them to take the bier to the chapel. When they had gone and the door closed behind them, Alberson spoke to the four captains. "The tale of what has happened will be long, so you just as well take your seats." Turning to look at the others in the room, he said, "Girls, refill our glasses, then fill glasses for the others. Captain Zackoro, if you and your friends will take a seat, we can get started."

When the twins tried to refill their own glasses, Janan put a stop to it. "Hold it right there. You young hellions have had your ration for the day."

The four officers stared at Janan and the twins, then turned their attention to Zack. When all had settled, the senior army officer stood before them but had a chair at his back. "Yes, this is the Captain Zackoro you have all heard rumors about, and yes, he took soldiers' justice in a fair fight on Quintson. But no, he did not deal justice to Antore. I know their tale, but I will let Captain Zackoro and Janan Jubedottir tell what happened before I came on the scene. I will finish the tale."

When the last of the tale was finally completed, Prince Almon was curled up on the big seat of the throne, asleep. Zack took in the sight and smiled, then said, "I think our young prince needs to see a bed, high captain."

Alberson also smiled at the sleeping boy, then turned to Minna. "Mam Minna, would you mind taking him to his rooms? And if you don't mind, stay by him. If you have need of anything, just ask the servants."

Minna nodded, then moved to shake the sleeper awake. "Come along, Almon. You are too big to carry."

After they had gone, all was quiet until one of the senior captains cleared his throat and said, "What now? You surely don't mean for that boy to be king."

"I mean exactly that." Alberson looked at each of the four, then continued. "Kemoc and I have both served good kings, and a good king is the best thing that can happen to the army. Under a good king, with a good army to back him, a realm can prosper. When a realm prospers both the people and the army prosper. For now, and for the foreseeable future, a regent will be needed until the boy reaches his majority. The regent will also have the job of overseeing the kingdom and the boy's training."

One of the four nodded. "Then you must be regent; a chamberlain cannot rise to such a post."

"I don't want to be king, nor regent. I am just an old soldier."

Another of the four grinned at him. "Alberson, being the senior surviving advisor to the king, I don't think you have a choice. Can you think of anyone you would rather see in that post?"

The jocular tone of the questioner caused a wry grin to come to the face of the old soldier, and the tension in the room eased. The tension eased further when Alberson said, "Why not one of you?"

"Oh no," said a third captain, "this mess was on your watch, so you get tagged for the cleanup."

"Very well. If I get stuck with the regency, you four move up to high captain and will be advisors to the regent. I am sure each of you have someone you can promote to take your place. I will stay in the army as its one general and will be in overall command of the army. I will not interfere with the high captains' day to day command. I will, though, advise."

Finally one of the four interjected a somber note into the proceedings. "There will be attempted coups."

Alberson's eyes twinkled as he said, "There are always coup attempts, but I doubt any of you made it to your present rank without having a spy or two in your employ. With those, and an elite guard, we should be able to manage any plotters. Having such a guard could have prevented what has happened, and our king might still be with us." There was amusement in the new regent's eyes.

"Now," the old soldier's eyes were again a-twinkle, "we will use this 'The King is dead. Long live the King' ceremony in the plaza before the castle. We will bury the reprobate in style, with a quarter of the army looking on, and with as many of our citizenry that can safely be accommodated."

When Alberson stood, all followed suit. Then one of the newly promoted high captains asked, "Who will guard the boy until we have found trustworthy men to form the palace guard?"

"I will ask Captain Zackoro, with his troop, to stay until things settle down and all arrangements have been completed. The four of you will have the harder task. You must forestall any coup attempts and start the rumors about the king dying of heart-stop. For the army, the rumors will be about how it will be a good thing that the regent is a past high captain, and of how the boy will be trained to be a worthy man and a good king."

The man asking the question had noted calluses on the hands that had held the wine pitcher. Walking over to Lee, he said, "Let me see your hands, girl."

Janan frowned, but Lee just grinned and complied. The soldier examined the placement of the calluses on her hands for a moment, then studied the grinning face before him. "You handle a sword with either hand." It was not a question.

Her grin widened. "Aye, and the same with a knife. I do a fair job with bow and spear too."

He looked around, assessing the rather motley band, which caused Zack to chuckle. Giving a friendly nod he said, "If you wonder about their weapons competency, captain, ask those who were with Gortson. And, sir, I have need of a messenger. A good one. I think you will find the man I have a mind to call on will do admirably for the captaincy of the elite guard."

The next day the twins went to check on Ivor, but on seeing them he became so agitated that they were asked to leave.

Lee was feeling downhearted as they walked back to their room. They had been assigned such a sumptuous room that they felt uncomfortable in it until they learned that it had been the room of one of Antore's concubines. After their laughter had died down, they settled in and enjoyed the big beds and the adjoining bath. They also tried to get used to servants.

"Sis, how am I to see Ivor if he goes nuts every time we walk in?"

"Why should you even want to go see the big stupid?"

"Oh, shut up and help me think of something. Do you think it would help if I went alone?"

Now Dee was not completely without feminine wiles. After

thinking for several paces she arched one brow at her sister. "Yes, especially if you would be willing to play a serving maid. I'll bet we could find you a gown to wear, one like those Zack made us wear. Then if I did your hair up like we did then, you could take him his meals. Let's go talk to those two women who keep trying to take care of us."

It was not long before the household servants got wind of what was going on, and they were having a gay time of helping. It was rare entertainment for those whose entertainment was somewhat limited.

After five days under the care of the palace healer, Ivor was feeling much better, if somewhat weak. The witch had ceased barging into his room, and Almon had been to see him almost every day. Ivor was still getting used to the idea that his young friend was a prince, and that he would one day be king.

A bit hungry, he was waiting impatiently for his noon meal when the door opened to admit a lovely young girl bearing his tray. She was a great improvement over the healer's male helper who usually brought his food.

The girl kept her eyes modestly lowered as she assisted him to sit up, and while stuffing pillows behind his back. Fortunately he couldn't see the eyes that were so filled with mirth. He was disappointed when she turned and quietly left the room. Soon she was back, carrying a tray containing a glass and a small jug of wine. Setting the tray on the bedside table, she poured a glass of wine and placed it on his bed tray. Backing away, she stood several paces back, her long lashes all but hiding the downcast eyes. As he began his meal, she folded her hands and waited quietly.

Eating slowly, Ivor kept glancing at the girl until he could stand it no longer. "Hello, I have never seen you here before. May I ask your name?"

The answer was very low, and she never looked up. "Leeta."

She was definitely not a witch, though she did have yellow hair. The hair fell almost to her narrow waist and was held in check by a bit of hair pulled back from each side of her pretty face, to be joined at the back with a bit of ribbon.

"That is a very pretty name for a very pretty girl." The smooth skin of her face turned rosy as Lee tried to contain her laughter.

"I am sorry. I did not mean to embarrass you." He hesitated slightly, then added, "My name is Ivor. Will you be bringing me my food from now on?"

Again the answer was low. "I was not told."

"Prince Almon is my friend; perhaps I can get him to order it so. Would you like that?" The girl's face bloomed from rosy to red. There was another thing Ivor was ignorant of. Dee and the two maids who had helped coach Lee were listening at the door.

Unable to stretch the mealtime any longer, Ivor finally let the girl take the trays out of the room. In the hall, the two maids took the trays, then all fled to the kitchens, where the four of them burst into laughter.

Twenty-four

From his treetop perch, the watch called down, "One rider coming, at speed. He leads a second horse."

Mathou motioned to two men. "Come along, we'll see who is in such a hurry."

When the three walked clear of the trees, they stopped and waited. The oncoming rider saw them and reined his cantering horse to a walk. When he had closed the distance, he stopped and held high one hand, the universal sign for a peaceful meeting. "I have a message for one Mathou, from Captain Zackoro."

Mathou returned the salute, then said, "You have found him, and under the rules of parley you have safe conduct, soldier. Climb down and lead your horse. We have water for both horses, and tea for yourself." Mathou managed a smile. "Who knows, we might even find some fodder for all three of you."

As they walked to the camp just inside the wood, the old woodsrunner kept his impatience in check. The walk to the camp gave time for most of the village folk to fade into the wood; thus, the messenger could not gain information. After both he and the messenger had a big mug of tea in hand, Mathou led the soldier to a log, where they both sat.

"You, my friend, need some sit down time on something that is not moving, and you can tell your message while you are resting."

The man set his mug on the ground, then undid the latch of a pouch he carried. From his courier's pouch he removed a rolled and wax-sealed scroll. The older man broke the seal and started deciphering the scrawled writing.

"Heyla, Mathou. All is well, thus far. Quinton and Antore are dead; Minna is safe and with us. We have made pact with the one remaining high captain and the chamberlain of the castle. Things have turned out to be a bit different from what was expected, so we will not be running for the wood. Nor is there likely to be any fighting, so you may return to the village. It would not be a bad thing, though, to keep a few good eyes on the plain. I sent you an ex-soldier, along with his wife and child. I hope they and Jokome arrived safe and sound and that you welcomed them. Please tell Doubson that I request that he return with the messenger. I have secured for him a new position in the army, if he wants it. Tell him that he will be captain of an elite guard within the castle. The choice is his, but if he comes it might be best if his family stays on at the village. If things work out he can bring them up later. I am sure you will see that his wife and child are well cared for. To ease any worry you may have, I tell you that one of my party comes from across the western Desolation and that Sallee should not have to put up with the likes of you. Zack."

Mathou reread the message, then sipped from his cup. "Tell me, messenger, what news from the city?"

The man had slipped from the log and was now using it for a backrest. "Strange doings, old man. The king died of heart-stop, so they say, and we buried him with honors. It seems we now have a crown prince and a regent to train him up. When I went to pick up this message there was a strange captain in charge of a very odd set of castle guards. Those guards included three warrior women who carried sword, knife and bow. With them was one foreign-looking young man and one old man; all of them were armed alike. There are changes in the wind, but all seems peaceful."

"Were you told to hurry?"

175

"I was told to hurry the message to you, so to keep up the pace I swapped horses often. I was told to deliver the message, then stay with you until I could bring an answer."

"Very well, young man, we will move back down the trace to our village, where you and your animals can get rested. I must talk to two men before I can send an answer, but I think you will enjoy your stay in our village."

The shy young woman had brought his lunch and was about as talkative as ever, so the fact that Almon had wandered in behind her was no problem.

"So, Your Highness, what is happening on the outside?"

"Oh, shut up, Ivor, or I will highness you with a club. How are you getting on?"

He chuckled, then said, "Well, that witch and her double have not been bothering me. Maybe she has gone away. I am getting stronger by the day, and I hope I can soon go back to the army."

"Witch? You mean the two that dress in leather and fight like a man?"

"Yes, that's the one I mean. I hope she is long gone from here."

It was very undignified of the prince to giggle, but giggle he did, then guffawed. Tears ran down his face as he tried to contain himself. Finally wiping tears and getting his breath back, he pointed at the man in the bed and said, "Are you insulting my sisters?"

"Sisters!" Ivor didn't notice Lee giggling into her hands. When Almon started slapping his knee and howling laughter, she put both hands over her mouth and ran from the room.

Finally Almon drank from the wine jug on Ivor's tray. The wine was watered, but it helped him regain control. Taking a deep breath he said, "I have two sisters. Well, half sisters, who are named Lee and Dee. Lee is the one you have been calling a witch, and her twin sister is Dee. Looks to me like you can't tell them apart any better than I can."

The stunned expression on Ivor's face almost set off the laughter again. "Ivor, your serving maid is just Lee with her hair let down, and wearing a gown."

176

"Lee…Leeta?"

"Yes, and her sister is Deeta."

At that moment Dee walked in and said, "Where's Lee? Zack wants to talk to our bunch."

The prince again giggled. "For some reason she just ran out of the room."

As she turned to leave Dee said, "She is just about as stupid as he is."

For the next while Almon had great fun telling Ivor the story he had wheedled out of Minna.

The servants had found Gregor some clothing to replace Doubson's uniform. From the nether regions of some chest they had come up with a set of hunting leathers. He was quite the well-dressed young man in leather and velvet. At his side, Lee was back in her now-clean buckskins, and she carried Doubson's uniform. She was also advising her sister. "Even with the new clothing, he is not very pretty. He just keeps on looking like a barbarian."

On his other side Dee had her arm possessively tucked through his. "You wouldn't know pretty if it hit you in the head. Just look at what you took up with! Pretty stupid."

Zack had sent word to Janan that she and the rest of his bunch was to meet him and Jube in the throne room, and that they were to bring the uniform. Almon trailed along behind.

Gregor was still laughing at the girls' antics when they walked into the throne room. In that ornate room they found Zack, Jube and Doubson in conversation with not only the regent and chamberlain, but an armed Jokome.

When Lee marched over to hand Doubson his freshly cleaned and mended uniform, Alberson smiled at her and said, "You and your men will be getting new uniforms, Captain Doubson. Until then you will wear your regular army uniforms." The regent glanced at Gregor, and his smile grew. "With your new uniforms you will be almost as resplendent as this young man."

Zack turned to his group. "Minna is getting anxious about Erick, so we will be heading home as soon as the palace guard is in place. Doub spent the whole of his trip up here thinking about the men he wants to enlist, so it should not be long. We won't leave until he gets his men organized, but again, that should not take too long."

Almon was looking up at Minna. "Do you have to go?"

She smiled at his doleful expression. "I have a son much younger than you waiting for me at home. Don't worry, Almon. You will be so busy that you will hardly miss us. Besides, Ivor will be here."

"Ivor will be going back to the army, and Kemoc wants me to learn a lot of stuff out of a bunch of old scrolls."

"It won't be all out of scrolls. There will be weapons training, which will include horses." Her expression was teasing as she added, "And you will need to learn to dance with girls."

"Durn girls." It was evident that he was not overly enthusiastic at the thought of dancing, then his expression brightened. "Maybe Jenny could come up here." Blushing a little, he added, "I would dance with Jenny."

The next day Janan walked into the room she shared with the girls and announced their departure would be the following morning.

"Tomorrow!" Lee was not happy. Then one thought boiled up from the turmoil in her head. "Go see Ivor tonight when he is alone."

It was very late when she snuck out of her room, wearing her dark and hooded cloak. The hall was almost dark; just a single torch burned at the far end. She was still some distance from Ivor's room when she heard a noise and froze in place. She was looking all around when she suddenly looked up. The hair on her neck stirred. A big, spider-like figure was descending from the high ceiling of the hall. On reaching the floor it moved into a shadow, and a second figure was coming down.

Lee moved quickly and quietly back in her shared room, where she touched Janan. Her mother came awake instantly. While the other two dressed, Lee took up her weapons and headed for the room occupied by Zack and Gregor. From there she made her way to the regent's room, while Janan woke Jube and Jokome.

They had planned for this, but no attack had come. Now that they were leaving, the newly formed palace guard was to have the responsibility. This unexpected attack was also coming from an unexpected direction. They would have to fall back on the old plan, and it was a good thing they had practiced for just such an incursion.

The eight defenders were waiting, but only Alberson was in the hall. They were just in time. The intruders had all reached the floor and were beginning to move. Alberson rapped on a door, which opened to the rest of his party. The torch Jokome and Janan each carried to a sconce gave more than enough light.

When the torchlight revealed a group of twenty well-armed men, Alberson stepped to the middle of the hall to greet their leader. "So, High Captain Obersson, you have decided for the throne. I thought it would be you."

The twenty were well trained and charged without hesitation. The odds were quickly cut in half by two flights of arrows. Then it was down to individual combat. Jokome's "toothpick" wrought havoc while Jube's spear worked point and butt. Janan's and the twins' blades were not as heavy as the attackers weapons, but had a lightning riposte. The hall rang with the sound of metal on metal and groans of the wounded and dying. There were few still standing when the last intruder went down. Their leader died when Zack's sword point swept across his throat, almost decapitating him.

Just four defenders were standing when the sound of running feet caused them to turn in defense. The new warriors turned out to be Ivor and Almon; each carried a long dagger.

"Have care, lads. Some of these may still be dangerous. Go get the healer and all the male servants you can find. Tell them to bring more torches." Alberson waved them back and added, "Ivor, after you have done that, please take the prince to your room and bar the door."

"But Leeta…"

Dee, who was trying to staunch the blood flow from her sister's side, tiredly said, "Pretty stupid." Then she yelled, "Your general just gave you an order, stupid, get going!"

As Ivor dragged the boy away, Minna arrived with an armload of cloth, which she started tearing into strips.

The newly formed palace guard arrived at a run. The whole battle had not lasted long, but the noise of the battle had alerted the guards on duty. With drawn weapons in hand, the guards began checking the fallen intruders.

The healer arrived with half the servants at his back. With a quick but professional look at the carnage, he pointed his two helpers to two of the intruders, then he went to work on Lee.

With the healer working on her sister, Dee slit her own trouser leg and began bandaging the wound she had taken, only to have Minna take the dirty rags out of her hand.

When Minna finished working on Dee she looked around for others to help and found that Jokome had pulled off Janan's trousers so he could work on her thigh wound. A further look around caused a quick grin to come and go, when Dee limped over to where Gregor was trying to bind up his own wounded arm.

"Here, give me that, stupid. You can't do that with one hand!"

"You are beginning to sound like Lee. Keep your insults to yourself, woman, or I will paddle your butt after we are wed."

"Hey, that sounds like fun!"

With another look around she found Jube and his spear leaning against the same wall. "You all right, old man?"

"Aye, just tired. I got a nick or two, or three, but old Meg has yet to be rid of me."

Zack talked as he applied a bandage to the left arm of Alberson. "How many of our opponents survived, and what will happen to the ones that did?"

"More than you would think. As for what to do with those that did, I will think on it. Antore made frequent use of the gallows, so we will want to find another punishment. These are soldiers led astray by a traitor. It requires thought."

Twenty-five

When she woke, Lee had an ache in her side along with a variety of other aches, pains and memories, some sharp and some vague. She remembered the blade she couldn't fend off, and of seeing it drawn back for another stroke, then seeing Dee's blade intervene. Vaguely she remembered Dee by her side, then the healer feeding her something bitter. Finally she noticed that someone held her hand.

She turned her head to find Ivor sitting by her bed. "Hey, witch, how do you feel?"

As bad as she felt, she had to grin. Then, in a scratchy voice, she said, "So Almon told you about me and Dee?" When his chuckle answered her question she said, "Oh, shut up and find me some water."

"The healer said you may not sit up, but he showed me what to do." Gently raising her head, he held a mug to her lips. "Now be careful. Take it nice and slow so you don't choke. You start coughing and that side of yours is going make you wish you hadn't."

When she quit drinking he eased her head back on the pillow, then lifted a dripping cloth from a pan on the bedside table. After wringing the excess water out he began washing her face. "Hold still. You have boogers in your eyes and in the corners of your mouth, and I want you clean before I give back something you gave me." Finishing the gentle but thorough cleaning of her face, he leaned down and gently kissed her lips.

The kiss left her without words, probably for the first time in her life, but the arm on her good side came up and hooked around the back of his neck. Her strength was not taxed when she pulled him down for a longer version of what he had given her.

"Still pretty stupid." Dee and Gregor stood in the doorway. "Don't you know you are not supposed to wrestle with a wounded warrior?"

When Dee limped over to plant a kiss on her cheek, Lee said, "Hey, I owe you one. If you had not taken him out, that cow-flop would have taken another swipe at me."

"Na, I still owed you one from the last time we got into a little fracas."

As the two grinned at each other, Minna came through the doorway. "All right, you two men get out of here. Dee and I have to get this young lady out of bed. She must be near bursting." Lee's face burned red as Minna continued, "Then she gets another dose of that sleeping draught."

Under the burning sun the old calvary sergeant had no pity on the four he instructed. Gregor had proven to the old soldier that he almost knew how to ride, but Dee, her mother and grandfather were training alongside Almon, and catching a full load of abuse from the old army veteran.

"Ye ride like two women, a boy, and one old man, which ye are. When I get through with ye, you will ride like sojers. Now see if ye can mount properly this time."

The dusty foursome managed to get in the saddle without allowing the horses to move away from them. " 'At's right, 'at's right. Ye do it quick so your mounts don't have time to sidle. Now, girl, take your mount through the course." As Dee started through the obstacle course her instructor turned red in the face and started yelling again. "Na, na, na, girl. Neck rein, neck rein."

The regent had offered horses, and since it would be quite some time before Lee could be moved, Zack had decided he wanted the entire group to learn to ride, which meant the twins, Janan, and Jube. Lee could not join in yet, so she, Ivor and Gregor were watching from the shade of a tree.

"Actually, they are getting along pretty well, but that old sergeant will never tell them so." Ivor grinned at the other two. "I was in a group of twenty he taught, and he has yet to tell any one of us that we know how to ride."

"I am getting tired of being left out things just because that healer won't tell Ma that I am well enough." Lee was disgruntled.

Ivor put an arm around her. "You are lucky I have to go through retraining. I will be seeing that old man all too soon, and that will be after the ground training to get me back in shape. I'm surprised Alberson hasn't already ordered me back to duty. Maybe Almon has been talking to him."

Actually it had been both Lee and Almon, and Lee had been trying to talk Ivor into getting out of the army. She wanted him to move to the village.

"Just think, Lee, you will get to take it easy on your way home, riding in the wagon with Minna and Jokome." Gregor was indulging in a little payback. Lee was still want to call him names.

"When will you be leaving?"

Lee ignored her tormentor and answered Ivor's question. "Three days from now." Then she added, "Are you coming?"

"I can't. I asked Zack about it, and he said I would have to serve out my time or desert. If I deserted, I couldn't stay in the kingdom. Besides, I don't know that I want to be a farmer or a hunter."

"Well, I don't know that I want to be a soldier's wife."

Ivor wisely didn't mention that he had yet to ask her to be a soldier's wife. He was in a quandary; he was too junior to be able to afford a wife.

While the "kids" bickered, the regent was talking to Zack. "Captain Zackoro, I wish I could do more for you and your troop. I owe all of you a great debt of gratitude, and I wish you would think about my offer."

"You have given us clothing and horses, general, and you are doing the best thing you could do for us. You are making the kingdom safe and prosperous. Just the fact that we don't have to worry about being attacked by the king's men is reward enough. As for me taking over the castle guard, you have Doubson. Look at what he has already done to safeguard Prince Almon and yourself. You can be sure there will be no more attacks via the battlements. Topping that is the fact that I have aged and have other responsibilities. We still worry about those western plains barbarians, so the village warriors need someone to keep them in shape."

The regent was still in his general mode when he said, "Perhaps I should post a garrison down that way to keep an eye on our southern border and the Desolation to the west of your village. Think about it, Zack."

"Hmm, it is tempting, but I don't think a group of young soldiers would make for a tranquil village. The addition of just one young barbarian has caused enough bickering. Several of the lads had their eye on the twins."

Alberson's eyes held a mischievous glint that was quite reminiscent of the spark often seen in the eyes of said twins. "And now you have Lenderson to worry about. I quite understand. I came from just such a village." He was silent for several moments, then said, "A solution has come to mind, captain; one that will solve some re-enlistment problems for the army. There are always those who will want to go back to the land. Some are older soldiers with families, and some are younger with very young children. Now a mounted troop of, say, four five-squads would be enough for a regular patrol, and if they are all family men the tranquility of your village would not be disrupted. Your villagers are trained to defend themselves, and if you were promoted to senior captain that would give you five captains with sixteen troopers of various ranks, and your band of irregulars, of course."

Zack started to pace, then to think out loud. "There would be no need to build a barracks if each man lived with his family. Since the soldiers would be busy it would take them a long time to build a home, unless the crown could see its way clear to use the money it would have taken to build barracks to hire help in the village. A sawyer's pit could be dug back in the wildwood. I have often thought the village homes could use floors. Maybe a smithy. We could expand the grain fields. Hmm." Zack looked up to find both regent and chamberlain grinning at him.

Then Kemoc said, "That is quite a town you are planning, captain." Zack's smile was a bit sheepish, then all three men laughed.

Finally Zack said, "All right, sir regent, you have convinced me; now all I have to do is convince the village."

When the cavalcade was about ready to leave, Ivor assisted Lee to her place on the wagon seat. Standing on the wagon wheel, he gave her such a look that Minna was hard put to keep a straight face.

"Leeta, will you wait for me?"

In answer, she leaned over, wrapped both arms around his neck and kissed him long and thoroughly. Coming up for air, she said, "I better not hear of you chasing after any of these fast city hussies, you hear, Ivor Lenderson!"

When Jokome chucked to his team, the young soldier had to jump down. The last Lee saw of him was when the wagon passed through the city's south gate. He was still standing in place. To be sure, no guard demanded a tax receipt as they left the city.

They stopped early that afternoon at the campsite on the plain. At the nearby stream the twins stood guard while the two older women bathed, then Janan stood watch for them.

Their next stop was at the camp in the edge of the wood, where a mixed contingent kept watch on the plain. The young women, who were the contingent's "bowmen," joyously carried off the four women to swap news while the men conferred.

"I think we can do without a full guard here." Zack and the leaders of the villagers were drinking tea while the cook worked on supper. "I think we can go back to regular patrols now. The regent has things in the kingdom under control, and we are in very good ordure with the crown."

The rest of the trip was by easy stages. Zack had told the watchers they could join the little cavalcade, but they, perforce, were walking. Minna and Dee left the others and disappeared into the wood, leaving Greg charged with the care of Dee's horse. Minna was not waiting; she wanted to see her son.

The welcome was almost riotous when the small cavalcade came into the village square. While preparations for a night of celebration got underway, those who had made the trip from the city, as well as those who had stood watch at the edge of the plain, thankfully settled back into their various homes.

The four men of Zack's group found a shady spot under a tree and sat with Mathou and the lead warriors of the village. After the proposal of the regent had been explained, the questions began.

Jube sat leaning against the tree's trunk, a look of vast amusement making his eyes sparkle. When the questions and answers had slowed to a halt, he let out a loud snort. "Look at the lot of you. You got worry lines on yer foreheads like a bunch of old women. Take a look at what we get, Mathou, ye old woodsrunner: twenty-five highly trained and experienced fighters and more. These men are all married, most with families, and want the settled life of our village. We get the good will of the crown, crown gold to settle these men among us, and maybe a saw pit back in the wildwood. I were talkin' with old Alberson, the regent, before we left, and he was talking about a forge down here. He liked the look of our swords when he first got a good look at them, and he told me that he has sent an agent all the way to the sea. The agent is to try to beg, borrow or steal a man who knows how they do that folding of metal to make those blades. Hey, this old hunter knows a good deal when he sees one."

Mathou turned a thunderstruck look on him, then said, "I had not thought of it in quite that light, Jube." He stared at his old friend while the silence created by the sudden turn in the discussion held. "You trust that yonker?"

"Aye, and for good reason." Jube stood and stretched before looking all around the group. "Now I am going to go put the old bones on a bed. Gotta be in shape for tonight, and if you don't announce at that get-together that we will be having new families moving in, you are all idiots."

The announcement that night caused quite a stir of excitement, but the explanations by Jube and Janan went a long way toward settling any worries the villagers had.

Only Lee was glum, despite the promises by her mother and her twin that she would soon be learning to ride. "Well," she thought, "at least I can ride with Zack to the city when he goes to report to the regent."

News from the city was sparse until a messenger rode in with dispatches for Zack. Along with a sack of gold and silver coin, the rider's pouch contained instructions for building the housing for the troop. Using the needs of the largest military family, each building would be made to that specification, and there was to be one extra accommodation.

When spring came the work went faster and was encouraged by the crown's sack of money. The buildings were completed, with a garden patch behind each. Additional grain fields were planted, and a pit was dug for the saw Jokome had brought from the south strapped to the undercarriage of his wagon. The first boards sawed were used to floor Captain Zackoro's new home. Those floors saw the many feet of those who came to see the wonder.

While all the busy commotion was going on, Jube had taken to watching Janan. She was unusually quiet as she helped with various projects. Even at weapons practice her condemnations were muted.

One evening Jube was sipping tea before his hearth while Megan mended a shirt by the light of a five-candle lamp. "Old girl, do you note anything different about Jan lately?"

"Took you long enough to notice, old goat. I think it has been too many years since you were a boy."

"What are you goin' on about?"

"Watch the young girls about the square. It doesn't matter if it is at a gathering or just an ordinary day. When one of them gets struck on one of the boys and can't figure out what to do about it, they won't chance being alone with that lad, but they mope around and watch him. In a group that includes the lad she will laugh and talk a lot and watch him out of the corner of her eye."

"So?"

"So watch your daughter when Jokome is in the village."

"Jan ain't no girl! She is a woman grown, with grown daughters of her own, and the twins don't do that foolishness."

Meg chuckled over her mending. "You must admit that the twins are not quite your average village girls. As for Jan, she changed after Antore. She didn't get to finish her girlhood. Now I think she is having

187

the same problems the young girls have. Like I said, watch her when Jokome is in the village. For that matter, watch Jokome. He is just as bad. They circle each another like a pair of strange canine."

Twenty-six

The evening finally came when Zack and Minna strolled over to see Janan and the twins. After tea was served Zack brought up the reason for their visit. "I am going up to Kingston to pick up my troop and to collect my new uniforms from the officers' tailor shop." He arched one brow at Lee before continuing. "And I think I should take one sword-swinger along to guard my back."

Janan chortled when Lee, without a blink, said, "When do we leave?"

"Well, now, I was thinking of male back guard."

"Then I'll guard *his* back. I'm going."

"Then again, it might be a good idea to have a woman along to talk to the women and children that will be in the caravan."

"It's nice to be wanted."

"Pay no attention to him, Lee." Minna gave her an understanding smile. "He intended to ask you if you wanted to come with him. You can see that Ivor of yours, and I want you to go see Almon for me."

Dee smiled sweetly. "By all means, sister, do go see Prince Almon. You can take him my greetings, and you can look around for a good husband. Just stay away from that pretty stupid soldier boy."

Lee's smile was just as sticky. "Speaking of boys, where is that weird-looking barbarian?"

"Oh, he and Carl are working on our new home. They have also decided to make their intentions known the same night."

"All right, girls, that is enough." The origin of the twins mischievous eye sparkle became obvious when Janan continued. "Besides, I don't remember Carl speaking to Liddy's parents, nor has Gregor spoken to me. It could be that all this house building is a little premature."

It was Lee's turn to chortle a long, giggling gurgle. "Hey, Ma, tell him no. I would love to see the look on his face."

The next day Zack and Lee were tying their bedrolls and saddlebags on their saddles when Megan walked up to Lee. "I'd like you to pick up a few things for me, Lee. Here is a list, and coins to pay for the things I want."

When Lee raised both brows over the things listed, Meg added, "Just make sure they are a little long and a little loose on you. I think you can figure out the right size, and I think russet and green shades would be about right."

"You up to what I think you are up to?"

"Let's just say that I am going to have a long talk with your mother while you are gone. There are extra coins in that sack should you want to pick up something for you and Dee, and for me, if you see something you think I might like. Jokome is up there; you might get him to help you with the prices."

"Dee and I made friends with a couple women who work in the castle; they would probably be more help than Jokome. Then, too, for the things we want they could probably outbargain him. 'Sides, he might get nosy."

"Jan, have you any idea how much you look like a young lass with her first boy?" Megan chuckled at the look that came to Janan's face, then she said, "and Jokome is just as bad."

The jaw that had dropped at Megan's words snapped back in place, then a chagrined look came to the younger woman's face. "Surely I was not that bad, Meg?"

"That bad." Megan slowly nodded her head, then her face became still. "Your boying and girling came to an abrupt halt when you met Antore. I hope you don't hold that against all men. After that you were pretty well isolated for a number of years. Of course, all this presumes that you are really interested in that no-good trader."

"Guess I must be if I was all that obvious. Maybe I should take a lesson from Lee and Dee."

Meg was chuckling again as she got up to go for the teapot, then as she was refilling their cups, she said, "I don't think so, they are one of a kind, doubled. No, I have something else in mind, something that should bring the pot to a boil." Her smile widened. "If all else fails you can always fall back on your daughters' ways."

"I don't know, Meg. I am a little old to be out hunting a man, and Jokome may not even be interested. On top of that I have a family, you know. The girls, you, Carl and Da, even Min, Zack and little Erick are my family. I really don't need a husband, and I am not all that sure about all this."

"Old! Huh, not an extra bit of flesh on you, nor a gray hair on your head, and you look more like an older sister to the girls than their mother. And, you know, that house of yours may be a bit big and lonesome when the girls move out. Don't worry about it. Just play it by ear and see what happens. Zack and Lee should be there by now, so it should not be very long before that caravan heads this way. Jokome may follow them in, hoping to do a little trading as they settle in."

The travelers walked their horses across the main square and pulled up before the military stables. A stable boy ran out to meet them, saluted the captain and said, "Your stall will be number three, sir."

Zack raised one brow. "And for the other horse?"

The young soldier hesitated for a long moment before saying, "Uh, sir, we are not supposed to stable civilian horses."

"Oh, and just where would you suggest we put a horse belonging to Prince Almon's sister?"

Now, this young man was a very bright young man. "In stall number two, sir." His answer was without hesitation.

"Very well, have the young lady's traps delivered to the castle servants. As for my stuff, are you familiar with the new troop that is being assigned to the southern border?"

"Yes, sir."

"Good, have my traps delivered to the commanding officer's quarters of that troop."

Lee glanced over at Zack as they climbed the stair to the main entrance to the castle. "I think both of us would find welcome in the castle."

"Probably, but I need to get acquainted with my new troop." He glanced up at the wide-open doors and the two soldiers there. "What would you bet that we get another argument from those two." Lee just grinned at him.

When they approached the doors both guards stepped forward and saluted, then one said, "Good afternoon, captain. Do you have an appointment?"

"That I do, lad. And the name is Captain Zackoro."

At the soldiers call, a young page came running. "Notify the captain that Captain Zackoro is here." The page left at a run.

While they waited, the soldier was eying Lee. He finally said, "Sir, armed civilians are not allowed in the castle."

Before Zack could answer, the second soldier laughed outright. "If you plan to disarm her, Dike, I plan to stay well out of the way." Chuckling, he added, "Is it Dee or Lee?"

She frowned at him, then shook her head as she answered, "Lee, but I don't remember you."

"You probably don't, seeing you were a little distracted at the time. You were busy bleeding all over the floor when I arrived, but I understand you got in your licks."

Eyes sparkling, she held up three fingers. "Three, by my count. Two with arrows and one with my sword; I don't know if any of them died. The cow-flop that got through my guard caught me before I could recover from downing that third one." Eyes still alight, she looked at the first soldier. "Do you think I should give this one a try?"

"Oh, no you don't, young lady. I don't want blood all over this floor, yours or his." Captain Doubson followed the page through the doorway. "Now you quit pestering my men."

192

"Hey, Doub, how is it with you? And before you ask, it's Lee."

"Aye, from the conversation I figured it was you." He turned and traded salutes with his contemporary. "Good to see you, Zack. You come for your troop?"

"Aye, and for my uniforms."

"Well, come along, the regent is expecting you, if not Lee. I imagine Prince Almon will be overjoyed to see her, though."

The first soldier was a bit miffed because the conversation's meaning was going over his head. "But, sir, the civilian is armed."

"Aye, lad, that she is, and she is one of a half-dozen civilians who will always be welcome in the castle armed." He nodded at the second soldier. "Gig, here, can explain it all to you."

It was a very disgruntled Lee who rode with Zack at the head of the caravan. Ivor had been in the field with his troop, and the regent had received an earful when he would not tell her where that troop was located. Zack had told her that the captain of Ivor's troop would be very unhappy if she showed up where they had set up camp, and if she did, Ivor's mates would guy the life out of him. On the other hand, Prince Almon was equally disgruntled, and Zack had received a bit of abuse because Minna had not come with him.

To the surprise of everyone, Alberson had assuaged Almon's anger by presenting him with a set of buckskins and requesting that he go south with the new troop to formally install them in their new station. Almon didn't even mind that he had to learn the speech he would deliver before both soldiers and villagers. He would give the speech standing by the fire pit in the village plaza. This he would do at the gathering on the night when the villagers gave welcome to the newcomers. None of this mattered to Almon; he would get to see Minna and Jenny. Of course, Zack did josh him a bit about dancing with Jenny.

It was noon, the fifth day of their trip, when the caravan circled their wains at a campsite in the woods, and Zack called Lee over.

"Why are we stopping, Zack? If we kept on we could make it in before dark."

"The drovers say their oxen are worn and must rest. We will start early in the morning and get in by midday. The women of the village wanted a half-day warning, anyway, so they could stock the new houses with enough food and water. In that way the new families will have something to cook while they settle in. Why don't you take Almon and ride on in tonight? That five-squad Alberson assigned to escort him back to the city can go with you."

Lee and Almon arrived to a warm welcome. Dee, Minna and Janan came out to meet them, then Megan arrived, to be introduced to Almon. Finally, as Meg was collecting her bundles from Lee, there came a screech, followed by a running Jenny. She promptly embarrassed Prince Almon by throwing her arms around his neck and kissing his cheek.

One of the squad made a move to protect their charge, but his captain caught his arm. "I don't think he is in any danger, Timon, since he and the girl are a bit on the young side for marriage." But the captain did frown when Jenny took Almon's hand and started leading the prince toward her parents' home.

Janan chuckled, then said to the captain, "Oh, just send one man along with them, captain, if you must worry. After that, if you brought along your squad tent, you can start putting it up," she pointed, "out in that meadow, then you can tell me how it is that Prince Almon was allowed out of the castle."

After the tent had been erected, Janan and the captain of the five-squad were seated at a table not far from the cook fire. The squad had the loan of stools and the table from the village folk. They had also been furnished meat, roots and other garden truck; the five soldiers were going to eat well. With their camp set up, and one of their number working up a meal, the captain had sent the last of his men to reconnoiter the village and to find the prince and his single escort.

"Well, captain, will you now explain the presence of Prince Almon down here?"

He smiled at Janan. "Alberson is an old soldier who knows how to use his assets to the best advantage, and he knows that his officers must know the war plans." The smile turned into a grin. "He called me in the night before we left and explained my escort duties to me, then he explained his reasoning. The boy does well with weaponry and with horses. To give him a rest from Kemoc and Kemoc's scrolls, the general decided the populace should get a good look at their prince, their future king. He wants the boy to make a good impression, so tomorrow night the boy will wear his buckskins. He will wear the silver circlet of his office, make his little speech, then remove the badge of office and join in the festivities. Now, when we return to the city he will wear buckskins, circlet, sword and knife, and will be noticed by the city folk. I suspect the pair of them, Alberson and Kemoc, will have agents along our route making sure the people know who is riding by and that he has been down south installing the new company that will guard our border. If the people follow and cheer as he climbs the stair to the castle, again led by the agents, I suspect it will not make the two of them unhappy."

Twenty-seven

The sun was overhead when Zack led his troop into the meadow where the five-squad assigned to Prince Almon had their camp set up. A large group of villagers stood nearby, watching the families climb from the oversized wagons.

Plans made before Zack and Lee had left on their trip made the settling-in process move quickly. An old sergeant, reading from a list, called out a family name, and a group of village women and girls stepped out of the crowd. They came forward to help the woman of the household and her children carry bundles to the house assigned to that family.

While this was going on the men of the village helped the soldiers unload the heavier goods from the wains, and to carry these items to the various houses. In a very short time the wains were empty, as was the meadow of newcomers and villagers. The only movement was that of the drovers tending their oxen and staking them out to graze.

Not more than a mark later, the old sergeant reported to Zack, who waited in the village square, "Captain, the girls are well pleased with the accommodations, and the villagers are gossiping with them like old friends. I think this is going to work out."

"Glad to hear that, sarge. I doubt that it is needed, but pass the word that there will be a get-together in the village plaza tonight. Folks usually wear their nicer clothing, and there will be dancing and other entertainments. Also, take my message to the captains of the troops. I want to see them before sundown at the squad tent in the meadow."

When the sergeant had saluted and gone, Zack saw Almon coming across the square, trailed by his three "watchdogs." Waving the three men off, he said, "Go get some food and get cleaned up for tonight. I will be coming over to talk with your captain after a while."

"When they were alone he led the boy to seats by the fire pit, where Almon said, "Zack, Minna has said that I could stay with you tonight. Will that be all right with you? I had to sleep in the tent last night."

"What I want doesn't matter, Prince Almon. You could commandeer any quarters you fancied."

"Aw, Zack, you know I wouldn't do that."

"I know that, son, and I think you need to hear a few other things from me, commonsense things that you won't hear from Kemoc. Now, then, it is not my place to instruct you, but who is to hear. It's just you and me, eh?"

Almon's grin was one of delight, and very boyish, as his friend and defender continued. "You will be King, Almon, and you have just a few years to learn the trade." As Almon's eyes widened, Zack added, "Yes, it is a trade, like any other. The smith learns hot metal. The trader and merchant learns goods and dickering. The tailor learns cloth, threads and design, and so on it goes. Almon, the king learns to lead his people and his army. Instead of dealing in metal or goods or cloth, kings deal in people, and it makes no difference if they are villagers, city folk or representatives of other lands. Don't look so woebegone. You will always have friends and advisors to help you. The biggest thing you must learn, though, is how to be a friend to your people. They must always know that you are king, but they must also know that you are always looking out for their best interest. In other words, that you are their friend. Now, then, that is enough of that serious garbage. You will get enough of that from old Kemoc."

Almon chuckled at the last statement, then said, "I don't know if I can remember all that, Zack."

"Don't worry about it. You can always come back for a refresher talk with me, and you know you will always find friends and a welcome in this village. Now, as to this speech of yours, I had a look at it and the instructions Kemoc gave you about how to deliver that speech. They are just right. You should have no trouble with it." Zack's eyes gained a glint. "You know, I think that old goat must have been raised in a village much like this one."

Zack glanced over the boy's shoulder as he laughed at Zack's description of Kemoc. "I have to go tend to some things now, but I see Jenny headed this way. You two can visit here while I see that your traps are delivered to Minna."

The five-squad captain was waiting for him with the inevitable tea when Zack walked up to the table by the tent.

When they had settled, Zack nodded toward the square where Jenny and Almon had gained companions their own age. "I think you can relax a little, captain. The boy is learning valuable things from those lads and lasses. The biggest danger to him right now is having a disagreement with one of the other lads. A little scuffle would do him no harm, and I suspect he has been taught bare hand defense. Any lad he scuffled with would be in more danger than Prince Almon. As for any other dangers, these people have lived on the borders for long, and they keep scouts out day and night."

"Aye, and my men tell me that there is no resentment in the village. Quite the opposite. I will keep my men armed, but they will not crowd the boy. We would not want the locals to think we don't trust them. The one problem is accommodations. He really should not be sleeping in our tent."

Zack smiled at the man's worries. "He will be sleeping in my house, Gorge, in my house. It is a long story, my friend, but my wife has mothered him for longer than the boy has been heir designate. One day when we have the time and ale for a good story, I will tell you all about it."

While the captain chuckled about his words, Zack looked toward the sound of horses hooves. Two riders were just entering the meadow; soldiers. Spotting the two officers, they rode to the camp and dismounted.

"Dispatches for Captain Zackoro, sir."

Zack returned his salute, identified himself and accepted the proffered pouch, never taking his eyes off the other soldier. Keeping his eyes on the second soldier, he said, "Are two riders now needed to deliver one message pouch?"

The second soldier came to attention and saluted. "Junior Sergeant Ivor Lenderson reporting for duty, sir. My orders are in the pouch."

Looking the dusty pair over, Zack said, "There is a creek just through those trees, and a good bathing pool. Take your spare uniforms, get cleaned up, then report back here. The cook will have a meal ready for you, and I will have read these dispatches."

The escort captain watched Zack go through the contents of the message pouch before asking, "Any problems?"

"No, no problems. You are to have Prince Almon enter the city the morning of the first day, which is five days from this morning. Even if you get a late start, three days should see you in the city by midmorning of that first day. The regent also sent a letter of explanation covering my new junior sergeant." Chuckling, he added, "Now I know why an extra house was built." He passed the letter to his fellow officer.

"Heyla, Zack. For the safety of my ears I am sending you Lenderson. His new rank may be a bit early, but I thought you needed a messenger. It will also help if you decide to make him your aide. He has an education and a good fist, so he can clean up that scrawl of yours before you send dispatches. Beyond that, it may keep Lee down there and off my back. Alberson."

While Zack was giving his new sergeant a few words of wisdom, the twins, their mother and Megan were doing things with hair and clothing. When it was time to walk to the plaza, Janan and her daughters were resplendent in new gowns. The twins wore different shades of blue while their mother wore a rich russet. As they had before, back in the valley, the twins had combed their hair to a long flow down their back with the small, controlling hanks of hair from each side joined and braided at the back of their head. Then they had done their mother's hair the same way.

Almon had found time to think about what Zack had said to him and had made a "royal" decision, one that suited him much better than the decisions that had been made for him. First he left the captain of his escort speechless by giving him a direct order and by not waiting for an answer. A bemused Jube received the same treatment.

That night "Prince Almon" stood by the blaze of the fire pit. Slender and erect, he wore his sword and knife with authority. With the royal circlet glinting silver on his brow, he projected his words as he had been taught. "I bring you greetings from the seat of the kingdom, and that is all of the speech written for me by the regent that I will use. I looked at it today, then threw it in the fire. I was to make a speech installing the garrison," he gave an exaggerated shrug, "but you have already installed them. I was to make a "welcome to the kingdom" speech, but it looks to me like you have already done the welcoming." He motioned to Jube. "So why aren't we dancing?"

As Jube's double-ended drumstick began dancing on his drum, Almon removed sword, knife and silver circlet to hand them to the waiting captain. While other musicians joined Jube, Almon drew Jenny to the center of the square to begin a slow pair's dance. Cheers and laughter followed them, then other dancers.

Back in the shadows, Zack was weak with laughing. Leaning over to speak into Minna's ear he said, "The little devil turned my words back on me, but I think he has won over our villagers."

Ivor had managed to find Gregor without the others noting his arrival, and Greg was all too willing to help with the surprise. They were all but hiding in the shadows, but Jokome had spotted them.

"Ivor! Where did you come from?" Taking in the mischievous expressions, he came to the correct conclusion. "Lee doesn't know you are here."

The young man from the western plains was all but sniggering. "Don't give him away, Jokome. Lee is about to get some of hers back. Why don't you stay by us and watch the fun?"

Jokome was laughing with the younger men when the two they awaited walked into the square, one on either side of their mother. Jokome's gasp made the other two spin around, then both of their mouths fell open.

"That can't be!"

Gregor stared for a long moment, shaking his head. "Got to be, Ivor. There are just three heads of hair like that in the whole village." He turned to the trader. "That is Janan, isn't it?"

Megan had saved them each a stool so they did not have to stand. Janan sat by Meg, while the twins sat side by side, drawing stares from every man in the area.

As soon as they were seated, Lee leaned over to whisper in her sister's ear. "I saw Greg standing with Jokome, and I would swear Ivor was with them. Look and see if I am seeing things; they are on the other side of the fire pit and a little to the left."

Dee, with quick glances, quickly confirmed what her sister saw, but held Lee down when she started to stand. "It's that very stupid soldier boy, all right, but you stay put. It looks to me that yours and mine are thinking to have a little fun. If you got the guts, dear sister, we can turn it back on them. You can claim him after the first dance. What say?"

The three men stood staring, not hearing a word of Almon's speech. When the dancing started, so did they, but Jokome was the one who had to speak for all three. "It appears that you three ladies are in need of a dance partner."

The young soldier suddenly had a blond beauty in his arms. Still unable to speak, he swung her out among the dancers. When Gregor danced away with the other blond, Jokome held out his hand. "It would seem that I have the honor of dancing with the beauty of the dance."

Janan's eyes were filled with the family sparkle when she joined him on the dance floor. Finally Jokome had to break the silence. "I knew the twins were pretty, but I had no idea they were lovely." He glanced down into dancing eyes. "Nor did I know that the beauty of the daughters was so much less than that of their mother."

"Why, Jokome, you could turn a girl's head with such talk."

The silence came back until Janan stiffened. "Uh-oh, I think my daughters have stirred up some mischief. There is a cool, wine-laced fruit punch being served over this way. Let's get a couple mugs and watch the fun. I just hope it doesn't come to blows."

When they each had a mug of the punch, they moved a little way into the shadows. After studying the dancers, Jokome shook his head. "I see nothing wrong."

"Well, I do. The wrong color gown is with the wrong man. It looks to me like the boys decided to give Lee a shock and got caught at it."

"Looks as though you will be having two word-takings to oversee."

"Make it three. Carl and Liddy will also make their announcement of intentions tonight."

Jokome suddenly leaned down and put a soft kiss on her lips. To his surprise, she pulled him closer and returned his kiss with interest.

"Well, I didn't think my pulling off your trousers would cause an excitement that would last this long. Maybe we should slip off and find…"

"Now you just hold on to your horses. Trousers are one thing, but underpants are another. If you think any man can get those off without…"

Jokome had put the tips of his fingers to her lips. "Quiet, woman. Let a man have his say before doing him the discourtesy of interrupting. As I was saying, if we slip off and find Jube, maybe we can make that announcement a four-way declaration of intentions."

Printed in the United States
32875LVS00006B/1-51

9 781413 757354